D0842689

2/33

TALL MAN RIDING

Also by Norman A. Fox
in Thorndike Large Print

The Rawhide Years
Reckoning at Rimbow

This Large Print Book carries the
Seal of Approval of N.A.V.H.

TALL MAN RIDING

NORMAN A. FOX

CLAYTON LIBRARY
6125 CLAYTON ROAD
CLAYTON, CA 94517

JUL 0 6 1992

Thorndike Press • Thorndike, Maine

3 1901 01746 8481

Library of Congress Cataloging in Publication Data:

Fox, Norman A., 1911-1960.
    Tall man riding / Norman A. Fox.
        p.   cm.
    ISBN 1-56054-190-3 (alk. paper : lg. print)
    1. Large type books. I. Title.
[PS3511.O968T35   1991]   91-16378
813'.54—dc20   CIP

Copyright © 1951 by Norman A. Fox.
All rights reserved.

The characters, places, incidents and situations in this
book are imaginary and have no relation to any person,
place or actual happening.

Thorndike Press Large Print edition published in 1991
by arrangement with Richard C. Fox.

Cover design by James B. Murray.

The tree indicium is a trademark of Thorndike Press.

This book is printed on acid-free, high opacity paper. ∞

For
BETTY and CHUCK PICHETTE
Old friends . . . Good friends

Contents

1. The Hunted

In the night, the sound of running horses brought Madden up in his blankets, and in the first awakening he wondered if this were some fragment of a dream, for there was only the soft sighing of the wind in the pines and the distant murmur of water come down off Tumbling Wall when he keened the restored stillness. He lay then, no longer sleepy; he lay until he heard the rolling thunder of the guns. Around him the pine pressed thickly, the interlaced canopy of boughs giving him only a wedge of sky, but he could see that the moon rode high, and he placed the time as midnight. He waited again for hoof or gun and decided that the sound had risen from the valley below, down there in the broad expanse of the Beavertail. The sound was a wraith, illusive in the thin atmosphere of this lofty land where the valley ended.

Madden got out of his blankets then, made a roll of them, pulled on his boots and swung his belt around his middle and got his sombrero; as simply as that he'd broken camp.

None of his motions had haste, but all of them counted. He got his horse from where he'd left it hobbled, forced the bit and took the saddle which had served him as pillow and swung it to the mount's back. He was ready then.

He stood for a moment, a loose and limber man, taller than most and made even taller by Justins and Stetson; he stood listening. His face was young, but it was the wooden face of one who'd diced with chance so often as to be contemptuous of chance; his eyes were slate gray, his features solid.

When he stepped up to leather, he put his back to the high, moon-glimmered wall that blocked off the valley's northern end and found his way downward through the pines, following a trail slippery with an eternity's fall of needles. Upon this spongy carpeting he made silent passage, descending always and stopping sometimes to let his horse blow. At these times he listened again, and once he thought he heard the guns, but he couldn't be sure. Whoever had ridden this way had started up the slope and then turned back; the hoofs that had drummed in darkness, disturbing his sleep, must be beating southward now. Sensing this, Madden was of a mind to bed down again, but something born of more than curiosity kept him riding.

Before he struck level ground, he broke free of the timber and looked down the valley, ethereal in the moonlight, vast and empty at first, until he saw the moving shapes, many of them, and heard the faint echo of a lifted cry. He sat his saddle here, straining his eyes and seeking a pattern in that movement below; and when he thought he'd found one, he began riding again, sometimes putting the horse down steep pitches with a calculated recklessness, shearing off distance.

He got to the level within an hour and found here a broken land of short-grass openness and shadowy coulees and dotting tree clumps, wild as all this far corner of Montana; and he wrapped caution about him then, avoiding the moonlight when he could. He moved steadily southward, and soon he had the sensation of riders all around him, though none showed. Somewhere in the night were hunters and hunted; he'd got that much of the pattern from above. But the hunters had fanned out, spreading themselves over the better part of a mile; sometimes he heard them calling one to another, and sometimes he heard the jingle of bit chains.

He attained the black maw of a clump of trees and sat his saddle again, looking out upon the trail which made a silver ribbon down out of the pine he had so lately quitted.

He sat here until he heard a rider come along, and Madden's only move was to lean forward and clamp a hand over his horse's nostrils. He was within a dozen feet of the rider as the fellow passed; he saw the man's face in the moonlight, tempestuous and turned taut and lupine by this night's work. The fellow wore denim, and his horse had been broken to the plow, if Madden were any judge; that was the surprising thing. Here was one of the hunters, for this one rode warily but without fear.

When he had gone beyond the reach of Madden's ears, Madden quit the tree clump and crossed openness and dipped down into a coulee, but again he had to freeze to leather and keep his horse silent; for again a rider came near, walking a horse along the coulee's rim. Madden waited out the man, letting the rider make distance; and then Madden followed the coulee. It was deep enough that little moonlight showed, and he dismounted and led his horse, putting each foot down carefully and stopping often. Another coulee bisected this one, a narrower, deeper coulee, born of some spring freshet that had raged itself to oblivion. At the fork, Madden risked a match and had his look at the ground.

He made his choice then, turning into the narrower coulee, and he felt the crawl of excitement as he groped along. His goal had been to find the center of that ragged circle of questing riders, and this was like gambling; he had made his guess how the wheel would turn; he had calculated the odds, but the rest belonged to chance. When a man stirred ahead of him, making a faint, betraying movement in the darkness, Madden knew that moment when the chips are raked in; it held always both fulfillment and surprise.

The man was only a voice in the darkness. He said wearily, "You can come and take me. I used my last bullet an hour ago."

Madden said, "Keep your voice down, you fool!"

He heard the quick intake of the other's breath; and because he knew how it was with this man, Madden knew also that he had to give him something that made for quick assurance. So he said, "I'm here to help." Then he asked, "They chasing anybody else besides you?"

"Just me."

"I couldn't be sure," Madden said.

The other had become a faint silhouette against the darkness. He asked, "Your horse fresh?"

"He'll do," Madden said.

"Perhaps we could hump up the side of the coulee. They're closing in, I think."

Madden moved forward in the darkness

until he came against the other's horse. He put his hand to its flank and found it soggy. "We sit, mister!"

"Sit! They'll have us hunted down inside an hour!"

"You've come as near riding that horse to death as you're going to. Show yourself and you give yourself away. We sit right here, mister."

He hunkered down then, holding his saddler's reins laxly in his hand; he heard the faint, furtive movement of the other man, and soon he sensed that the fellow was crouching, too. The minutes ran on, piling up a silence that was broken only by the soft movement of the horses; but always Madden was listening. After a long while, he heard movement on the coulee's rim above, and a man's voice said clearly, "Watch yourself there, Tom!"

There were at least two of them above, and Madden came to a stand then and got his hand over his mount's nostrils once more, and because he wasn't sure whether the hunted man might not be too panicky to remember, he risked a whisper in the darkness. He saw dimly that the man was standing, too; they waited out the endlessness of this until sound moved away from the coulee and was lost in the night.

After that they crouched again, but the fear

of the other had been whetted by that inter-
lude of danger; his fear was in the air and
reached out to Madden and was like something he could have taken in his hand. The
other said, "Don't you think we'd better be
moving? This mount of mine must have his
wind back by now."

Madden asked, "What do they call you,
mister?"

"Willard. Rex Willard."

Madden started. "Of the Warbonnet?"

"Yes," Willard said. "I'm Tucker Ordway's son-in-law. Do you know him?"

"I know him," Madden said; and he began
to laugh then, deep inside himself, keeping it
silent. After a bit, he said, "I've just shaped
up a quirly. I'm going to light it. Don't go
jumping when I show fire."

He thumbed the match to life and cupped it
quickly and got it to the bit of twisted paper
and tobacco. In that brief instant he had his
look at Willard and saw that he was young and
slight of build and almost sallow in his pale-
ness, a reed of a man in a corduroy riding suit;
and the laughter bubbled in Madden again
and had no humor in it.

Willard said, "I don't remember your face.
And I've been trying to fathom how you could
have been in this end of the valley without my
running across you earlier today."

"I came down off the Wall."

Willard said, "Off the Wall! I find that mighty hard to believe!"

Madden shrugged. "I don't give a short snort in hell whether you believe or not."

Willard said, "I didn't mean to insinuate. I'm jumpy, that's all. They kept shoving me toward the Wall for hours. I could see their game. If they got me down to this end of the valley, they were bound to corner me."

"What's the ruckus about?"

"They're some of the younger hotheads among those settlers who are camped outside Sawtelle. But perhaps you don't know about them. It's the old trouble between cattleman and plowman. Warbonnet isn't popular in town. I had to go in today on business. I met this bunch just this side of Sawtelle. First it was words. When they took to chasing me, I think it was to have been just a lark. Then they got blood in their eye. It's been hare and hounds since late afternoon. They've kept me cut off from Warbonnet's gate."

Madden pinched out the quirly. "Well, we'll get you there, Mr. Willard."

He came to a stand then and said, "This way," and began leading his horse back along the coulee. When he came into openness, the moon still showed, but it was dropping toward the western rim of the Beavertail and a

16

cloud rack now obscured its face. He stood in the night, in the silence, and then he looked toward Willard and asked, "Think you could perch behind another man's saddle?"

Willard said, "You've got me pegged as an Easterner. That doesn't mean I can't ride."

Madden walked to Willard's horse and took the reins from Willard's hands and wrapped them about the saddlehorn. Swinging his sombrero off his head, Madden slapped the horse across the rump and sent it galloping in blind panic.

"Are you crazy?" Willard demanded. "You've left us with just one horse to carry the pair of us! I tell you, those men might still be around here."

Madden stepped up to saddle and sat looking down at Willard. A good-looking enough face, Madden decided, and a stubborn chin, maybe, but a man needed more strength than Willard showed to be Tucker Ordway's son-in-law. "They *are* still around," Madden said. "But they'll chase your horse awhile. Thank your stars that you've had stubble-jumpers on your trail instead of cowboys. Good men would have tracked you down long ago." He reached and fumbled with the ties holding his bedroll and let the blankets drop. "Now climb up here behind me and we'll make ourselves scarce while they're tailing an empty saddle."

He kicked one foot free of the stirrup and gave his hand to Willard; and when the man was seated behind him, Madden urged the horse to a trot, facing north again.

After a while, Willard said, "Warbonnet's gate is the other way."

"I know it," Madden said. "And *they* know it. In the name of sense, man, what would you do if you were in their boots and lost a Warbonnet man you were hunting? Where would you go to head him off?"

Willard said, "You think me a fool, don't you? And the damnable part of it is that you're right!"

"Yeah," Madden said and put his bitterness into it. His face turned bleak. Then he said, "When a man travels across country, he carries a hammer in his saddlebag. That's to let down fences and staple them up afterwards so he won't spend his days hunting gates. I'll get you onto Warbonnet land. But we'll travel a wide circle first. And we'll be heading just opposite to the way they'll figure we'll go."

They moved into a clump of trees then, the darkness coming down to smother them, and Madden put his free hand before his face, wary of branches. He walked the horse and got through the grove and came out upon its far side; and the three were there, sitting their saddles. There had been a dozen of the hunters,

Madden had judged from the slope above, but they had broken into groups, and these three had chosen this sector to scour. And now, as suddenly as this, Madden was into them.

If they had heard him coming, they had had scant warning. He judged that they had been moving up to this last moment, for their surprise was as great as his. Thus the advantage belonged to nobody, and Madden's move toward his gun was instinctive. He got the weapon into his hand and saw the glint of dying moonlight on the gun-barrel of one who was so close that he could have touched the fellow. Madden fired first, the shot lifting the man from his saddle and flinging him back over the rump of his horse.

Madden wheeled his own mount then; he felt Willard's arms tightening around him, and he thought: *"Leave my gun-arm free!"* and found that he'd shouted it. He was in the midst of a maelstrom of rearing horses, and he clouted out with his gun-barrel, striking for a man's head but hitting his shoulder. Still, he'd emptied a second saddle. He had a brief, confused impression of one man down in the grass lying still, another down and writhing, and horses squealing in the night, one racing away madly. That was the third man's; the fellow had got a quick bellyful of this kind of fighting.

Madden fed spur steel to his own mount then, for if there had been three hereabouts, there might be others and they would be drawn by the gunfire. He thundered toward the north, heading for the timbered slope and not bothering to be wary. He kept the mount at a hard gallop until he was into the timber. Then he spilled down from the saddle and dragged Willard to the ground and burrowed far into the brush, hauling the horse after them.

"We sit again," Madden said and hunkered down.

"You killed one of them!" Willard said, his voice shaken. "I'm sure of it."

"Hell," Madden said, "you're alive."

They sat here waiting while the moon slipped behind the western hills and the darkness before dawn cloaked all the land; they waited till the dawn showed red, limning the Beavertail's farther wall; and Madden rose stiff-jointed and said then, "We ride."

He came boldly out into the openness, Willard behind him, and he cut across country and found that country empty of riders. Dew bediamonded the grass and meadow larks made their caroling and the valley lay green and peaceful before them, and the night was something remembered as unreal and hazy, given the lie by sunlight. Madden rode until the strands of Warbonnet's wire glimmered in the early light, and he brought his horse to a halt before that wire.

"You can roll under," he told Willard. "From here on you walk. It isn't far."

Willard slid down and stood dazedly, the marks of exertion and excitement showing in his face. He looked at Madden. "You aren't coming to the ranch?"

"Not today," said Madden and let the silent laughter bubble. "I'd have seen you to the door last night, just to be sure you were safe. But you're safe enough now."

Willard said, "I know I owe you my life. If you ever need a friend, come to Warbonnet. Would you mind telling me your name?"

"Madden, mister. Lucky Larry Madden."

Willard made a groping gesture with his hands, his eyes showing how deep-striking this was; and Madden said, "I'll take my pay for last night's work when you tell *her* about it, Willard. But there's one thing you've got to get straight before we part. I hate your guts, mister. I bought in last night because anything that happens in this valley from here on out is part of my business. That was before I knew your name. After that I saved you because I wanted your hide whole. If anybody tacks it to the wall, it's going to be me. You can tell her that, too!"

21

Willard said, "Wait a minute — !"

But Madden was whirling his horse about, and Willard's voice was lost to him as he raised the horse to a gallop and rode away.

2. Wolf and Coyote

At sunset Madden came to Sawtelle, and behind him then lay all the day's long riding, for the valley stretched thirty-five miles southward from Tumbling Wall, and Sawtelle lay at the valley's end. Thus Madden had paced Warbonnet's wire in the morning, traversing a country broken by coulees and hogbacked ridges and seeing none of the riders of the night. By noon he had off-saddled beside a creek beyond Warbonnet, and he'd rested himself and rested his horse, for he had long ago learned that the best way to cover distance was the slow way. After that he'd found leveler country and much wire and many a tarpapered shack. These were new upon the floor of the Beavertail, and these he smiled upon, though he was rangeland born and hated the scarring made by a plow. But he saw these homesteads as a relentless tide rolling northward out of Sawtelle, rolling northward to lap at the borders of Warbonnet.

He used his hammer often in the last miles, letting himself through fences, but always he restored the staples and always he lifted his hand in friendly fashion to any plowman he saw. Once he had a dipper of water at one of the shacks; a gaunt woman served him, a big-eyed child clinging to her skirts. She gave him hospitality but little of friendliness with it; he wore range garb.

His pacing shadow was long when he sighted Sawtelle, and the dusk was flowing down from the hills, the sun dying in flaming beauty behind those hills; but here at the south end, the valley had broadened out and the hills were distant and Sawtelle lay in openness. Before the town stretched a sea of tents, tattered and dull gray, the smoke of cook fires rising. Here dwelt the new settlers, the ones who hadn't yet located, and from them had been recruited the force that had harried Rex Willard through the previous evening and night. Madden wondered about the one who lay dead in the shadow of Tumbling Wall.

The town was a double row of buildings facing its one real street, with other buildings backing these and strewing the flat without reason. Ancient cottonwoods threw reaching shadows, their leaves whispering, and the first lamps blossomed and cast yellowness from doorways and windows, and men made ghostly shapes in this half-light hour. Madden rode into the street and went unerringly to the

24

livery stable and left his horse there. He had asked much of the horse in the last twenty-four hours, and his orders for its care were meticulous.

He took his saddlebag and came to the boardwalk and stood in Sawtelle's midst, a tall man done with his day's riding, and he knew that he should find something in this moment — something of fulfillment or nostalgia or anticipation — but he was empty. He supposed this was because of his tiredness. All his thinking was lax, and he felt lazy, and it was a luxury just to be standing.

He went directly to the Ogallala House and climbed the hotel's steps and bobbed in through the lighted doorway. The long gallery fronting the building had a scattering of chairs, and a few men lounged in these; the glow of their cigars made so many slow-moving fireflies in the darkness beneath the wooden overhang. Madden crossed the lamp-lighted lobby and spun the register around and put his name to it. Over the space for address, he poised the pen, giving quick thought to this, and then, his lips quirking, he added: "Circle M Ranch, Sawtelle." There were very few entries in the register; he didn't have to turn far back to find the name of Ames Luddington — San Francisco. Luddington, he saw, had registered ten days before.

The clerk was new here, a boy who looked as though he might be dying of consumption, and he gave Madden no more than a glance as he tendered him a key. In an upstairs room, Madden at once raised the window, then washed the dust of the trail from himself; he had dry-shaved at his noon camp. He lay upon the bed for a while, letting the tiredness quit his muscles, and then he went down to the hotel dining room and had his supper. Some were strangers at the tables — Sawtelle had grown a bit — but he recognized Syd Baxter, the blacksmith, who dined with his scrawny wife, and Jess Barker, who ate alone; and both of these recognized him. Barker came over afterwards.

"Long time no see, Madden," Barker said and made no offer to shake hands. "Must be two or three years, ain't it?"

"Five," Madden said.

"That long?" Barker said. He was a gangling man whose clothes didn't seem to fit him; he had a weak face, and his eyes never met another man's, and he'd had no occupation a name could be put to. But now he wore a deputy's badge upon his faded vest.

Seeing this, Madden said, "Who pinned that on you?"

Barker at once turned guarded. "Yellow Lodge, of course."

26

"Hell," Madden said, "even the county seat wouldn't get that careless!"

Barker said, not putting any real force behind it, "You lookin' for trouble, Larry?"

"Not yet," Madden said. "And not with anybody cut so close to the ground as you."

Barker said, "You got no call to be snappin' at me," and turned and walked away. Madden fashioned up a quirly and had a second cup of coffee and put his speculation upon Barker and his badge for a brief while. Then he went out from the dining room to the street. Sawtelle was livelier; the boardwalks echoed to booted heels — those would be from the ranches, Hashknife and T-Square and Rocker-S and the others strung along the Beavertail's eastern wall — but the heavy boots of homesteaders were here, too. The mercantile across the way was alive with light and movement; horses waited patiently at hitchrails. Madden stood watching all this; and then, knowing where he had best go, he started along the planking for Pearl's Palace.

Five years of weather had dimmed some of the garishness of the saloon's high front, but the place had a personality and the personality had grown more blatant. Sound boiled out through the batwing doors, and in his mind Madden likened this to a bucket of garbage being dumped into the street, for the sound

27

had a taint to it; it was raucous and unrestrained and made of too much liquor. Inside, the room blazed with light from cutglass-festooned lamps, and tobacco smoke lay piled in the air. A bar ran the length of the big room, and in the sawdust-strewn expanse before the bar there were gaming tables and spaces for dancing; the professor's piano was shoved against the far wall.

Madden came up to the bar and had a cigar and wrapped himself in aloofness, scanning the bar mirror through half-lidded eyes. Men eddied around him, busy with their own pleasures, all but one — a lithe, dark-skinned youngster, girlish of face, slight of form, who stood with his back to the bar, his elbows propped on the mahogany. With one hand he held a coin, fingering it, turning it over and over. A Mexican, Madden judged, though the youth wore gringo range garb. His guns were tied down and his eyes were death's, and his presence here surprised Madden, for the killer breed had walked wide of Sawtelle in the old days.

The youngster paid him no noticeable heed, and Madden fell to scanning the crowd by way of the mirror. It took him a while to locate Luddington; the man was at a poker table, but shifting dancers kept moving between the table and the bar. Luddington was wearing a narrow-brimmed black Stetson, his concession to cow country, but his suit was gray and of San Francisco cut. His long, strong face looked horsy in the lamplight; he had no more than a casual interest in the game, and his boredom showed in his eyes. He was a man passing the time away and learning the town while he was at it.

The other two at the table were also known to Madden, for one was Cibo Pearl himself, fat and greasy and looking for all the world like a black-clad toad. Mace Stroud, the land locator, sat next to Pearl, a big-handed, big-bodied man, his ruddy face showing that he'd drunk too much tonight, his voice lifting above the professor's pounding. Looking at the two, Madden reflected that you could tell a man by the way he played poker. He watched the reckless bluffing of Stroud and the cautious playing of Cibo Pearl, and he thought: *Wolf and coyote.*

The woman stood so unobtrusively behind Luddington, one hand on the back of his chair, that she had escaped Madden. He saw now that she had black curls, piled high, and that time had not dealt too kindly with her; it took much paint and powder to keep the etchings of adversity from showing in her face. It was the roundness of her upper body, revealed by a tight-fitting silk dress, that told

29

him how young she was in years. He guessed that she was the latest of Cibo Pearl's women, and he wondered about this one; she seemed different somehow.

He watched the game until his cigar had burned down, and then he strolled over to the table. Stroud spied him first, and the land locator slapped his cards face down and came to a violent stand, thrusting out his huge right hand. "Larry Madden!" Stroud shouted. "By thunder, it's good to see you back, boy! Put 'er there."

Madden shook hands; and Cibo Pearl looked up lazily, not offering his hand, and said, "Lucky Larry . . . Which has it been, good luck or bad since we saw you last?"

Madden said, "Fair to middling." There was a faint aroma of perfume about Pearl that sickened him.

Stroud said, "Shake hands with Ames Luddington, Larry. He's newly come. Closemouthed gent; we can't get a peep out of him about his business."

Luddington stood and extended his hand. "Madden, is it?" he asked and kept his face straight.

Madden shook hands, looking hard across Luddington's shoulder at the woman. Cibo Pearl only riffled chips with his fat fingers, saying nothing, and it was Stroud who spoke

30

up. "Meet Reva, Madden. She sings here for Cibo. You'll like Reva."

Madden nodded to her and said, "I'm pleased to meet you."

She smiled at him, and in that slight parting of her lips lay warmth and a quick calculation and the shadows of questions unasked. "Do you dance, cowboy?"

Madden grinned. "I'm too strong with alkali tonight."

She nodded, dismissing him; he had made his refusal yet spared her her pride, and he had her gratitude; he knew that. She moved away from the group, and he liked the way she walked; she flowed among the dancers, touching no one of them. He felt eyes and found the lithe Mexican at the bar appraising him; the coin rose from the youth's fingers and came down to be caught, the youth's eyes never leaving Madden. Jess Barker came in through the batwings and had a listless look around and moved out again, and Stroud's voice reached through to Madden.

"Sit down! Sit down!" Stroud boomed. "We'll deal you a hand. Luddington, I warn you. This hairpin has more luck than ten men."

"Some of it good — some of it bad," Pearl said and smiled.

Madden shook his head. "Not tonight. I'm

that tired that all cards would look like the three of spades."

He turned then and left the saloon and walked the boardwalk back to the Ogallala. The night lay warm with August's warmness; he took one of the chairs on the gallery and was pleased to find himself alone here. He lifted his long legs to the railing and spun up a cigarette and began his waiting. He made his bet with himself that Luddington would be here within the hour; Luddington would play it like that, carefully, not hurrying away from the poker table too soon, lest either Stroud or Pearl sense that his departure tied to Madden's coming.

Horsemen stirred the dust, clopping softly along the street, and someone cramped a wagon's wheels hard, turning the wagon about; and all of the night sounds and smells and sights were around Madden as the minutes marched. The hour ran nearly out, and a man came along the boardwalk and paused beneath the railing and peered up and said, "That you, Larry?" But it was Stroud.

"You look well fed and prosperous, Mace," Madden said.

Stroud's chuckle sounded from the shadows. "It's not like it used to be, Larry. We've got Warbonnet on the run now. Do you know that old Tuck Ordway ain't showed his face in

Sawtelle for over a year? I've got home-steaders located half the length of the valley. They'll be tearing down Warbonnet wire in another month."

"And every one of them's paid you to locate land," Madden said.

"Hell, it's better than that, Larry. I've or-ganized them; they pay me to do their think-ing for them. I'm running notices in every farm paper in the Midwest. I'm going to be a big man here, feller."

"And if you get twice as many settlers as you've got homesteads — ?"

"That's their risk," Stroud said. "Look, Larry, you've got as much reason to hate Tuck Ordway as I have. I could use a rider who can be frisky with a gun when he needs to be. Fighting pay and found, Larry. How about it?"

"I'd sooner herd sheep," Madden said very carefully. "I'd sooner sell my saddle and go swamping in a livery stable."

Stroud looked up at him, startled to silence. Then: "There's no call to be sore, Larry. Not at me."

"Git!" Madden said. "Get on up the street! Do you think I'd tie up with *you?* Any fight between me and Tuck Ordway is private."

Stroud said evenly, coldly, "You're making a bad mistake, Larry." And he moved on then.

Madden spun up another cigarette and when he raised a match to it, he found that his hand was shaking, and he thought: *I've done too much riding.* He decided then to go to bed and let Luddington find him in the morning. But he waited out the cigarette and was just grinding it under his heel when someone waddled to the gallery and took an empty chair beside him. This was Cibo Pearl, and Madden thought: *First the wolf, then the coyote.*

Pearl said, "Unseemly warm," and fished inside his coat pocket. "Cigar?"

"No," Madden said.

Pearl sighed. "Nice to have you back, Larry. Queer that we three should meet tonight — Mace and you and I. Mace hasn't been in the Palace for weeks — too busy with his farmer boys. But there we were, all of us — three men who carry Tuck Ordway's mark."

Madden said, "You can forget that, Cibo. Lick your own wounds any time you like, but leave mine alone!"

Unruffled, Pearl asked, "You ever been inside Warbonnet's ranchhouse, Larry?"

"Never!"

"I was there once. The old fellow sent for me. It was after he'd had his crew smash my wheels that time, because he'd figured they were braked. Ordway has a big oil painting of himself hanging over his fireplace. It was done by some artist from the East, one of those folks Corinna used to bring home for the summers between school sessions. You should see it, Larry. The old devil looks as though he could step out of the frame and breathe fire in your face."

Madden arose. Pearl's perfume was in his nostrils, and he could see the white glimmer of the man's waistcoat. "I haven't slept in a bed for two weeks," Madden said. "I'm going to hit one now."

"Have you got a stake, Larry?"

"Look," said Madden, "what in hell is that to you?"

"I was thinking," Pearl said. "A man with your kind of nerve and luck could maybe get into Warbonnet and out again. With that oil painting under your arm. There'd be ten thousand cold, round dollars for you, if you made it. That, and half the fun we'd have afterwards."

"Half the fun?"

"I want to hang it over my bar," Pearl said. "I want to hang Tuck Ordway there, so that every drunken bum who parades in can lift a toast to him, if he wants, and every percentage girl he'd like to run out of town can thumb her nose. Maybe we won't have to lick our wounds, you and I, after we make that kind of fool out of Ordway."

Madden reached then, a boiling anger in him, and he got a hold on Pearl's collar and heaved the man to his feet and spun him around. Madden said, "There was something I always wanted to do when I was here before, but I never rightly had an excuse. You always stopped short of that, Cibo." And he struck Pearl then, his fist arcing to slam hard into Pearl's moon face, spilling the man backward over the gallery railing.

Pearl hit the boardwalk hard and lay silent for a moment, and in that moment Madden supposed he had crippled the man or rendered him unconscious and didn't care. Then Pearl arose, spitting and hissing like a cat, and made off down the boardwalk, limping slightly. Madden watched him go and stood then, his chest heaving and his knuckles still tingling and his anger smoldering.

He was this way when Ames Luddington climbed the gallery steps and said from the corner of his mouth, "Room twelve — upstairs," and vanished into the lobby, leaving Madden to turn and follow.

3. One Man's Way

Luddington's room was like Madden's, a creaky cubicle holding a bed and a chair, and a bureau with pitcher and bowl and lamp; and at this late hour the room held also the piled-up heat of the summer's day. When Madden eased into it, Luddington was sitting on the edge of the bed, staring thoughtfully at the lamp with its halo of winged things circling it. Madden moved at once to the lamp and extinguished it, saying, "You'll get no sea breeze in this part of the world, Ames. If you want to be able to sleep, you'll do without the light."

Luddington's interest instantly sharpened. "Is it that, or are you afraid of being targeted?"

Madden moved to the room's one window and had a look from it and saw that it commanded a view of the street and was high enough above the roof of the gallery that an eavesdropper would do little listening if one ascended the gallery. Sure of this, he raised the window a few inches; and the sounds of Sawtelle came into the room, but they were remote, diluted by distance.

Turning to face Luddington, Madden grinned. "How much did they clip you for tonight?"

"The poker game? About eighty dollars, I guess."

"That woman, Reva, wasn't standing behind you so she could stroke your hair. Her game was to signal your hand to Cibo. A flick of an eyelid, the lift of a finger. You might as well have been playing with transparent cards."

Luddington said, "I surmised as much," and smiled faintly. Stripped of his coat, he seemed both heavy-framed and loose-jointed, a big man relaxed; yet even now there was power to him, a driving force leashed for the moment. "When I work, I work hard, Larry. When I play poker, it's just for fun. Besides, one isn't asked to sit in again if he's too lucky."

Madden took the only chair and turned it around and straddled it. "You got in ten days ago, according to the register. That made a good, safe margin. I rode all the way. I hankered to see a lot of sagebrush and sky."

Luddington said, "I figured you'd show up from the south. I kept an eye on any dust in that road."

Madden shrugged. "I circled around to the

38

north end of the valley. In the old days, I always wondered if a man could bring a horse down off Tumbling Wall. I was too busy then to find out."

Luddington showed his surprise. "I've done some riding in your valley. That looked like a sheer cliff to me."

"There are game trails. And some easy slants, if a man's careful. What's the news?"

"About the mine?"

"That isn't what I meant, but it will do for a starter."

"I had a letter from the office yesterday, Larry. About all they've had to do is bank your checks for you. Expenses are being paid as fast as they accrue. You show a balance right now of a little over one hundred thousand. Don't fret about the Ophir; you really struck it rich."

"Anyone wondering about Old Man Midas?"

"A strike as great as yours causes curiosity. The Arizona papers have played it up big and reporters have been around. We give them all the same answer: an Eastern syndicate owns the Ophir. Your name hasn't been mentioned."

Madden smiled. "And your little job — ?"

"I had to go all the way to Washington, D. C., for my facts," Luddington said.

"That was a pretty loose assignment you handed me, Larry, finding the chink in Tucker Ordway's armor. That meant I had to be a detective first and a lawyer afterwards. But I've done the job for you."

He swung his long legs to the floor and crossed to the bureau and drew from one of its drawers a bulging briefcase which he brought back to the bed. He moved softly for so big a man; the springs creaked under him. "Can you stand a surprise, Larry?"

"I've had them, good and bad."

"Tucker Ordway never filed on Warbonnet. He doesn't own an inch of that land. Not legally."

Madden said, "I'm not surprised, Ames. Tuck was a Texan. He brought his herds north and settled on Montana graze. Few of his breed bothered to do anything in their day but squat on the land and hold it. When the homesteaders began coming in, some of the cattlemen went through the motions of filing, just to play safe. Some had their cowboys take up land, then sign it back to them. Tuck Ordway was too confounded independent for his own good!"

Luddington's eyes took on a hard shine, and he said, "You've got him, Larry! You've got him good! Warbonnet is actually public domain. There's a federal marshal on his way

40

to Sawtelle right now. I made the arrangements for that while I was East. Once he gets here, Ordway can be evicted and the land thrown open for filing."

Madden said, "You keep that marshal on ice till we're ready to use him. There's got to be a time and a place."

Luddington shook his head. "If we wait too long, somebody else is going to close in on Warbonnet. If this fellow Mace Stroud had the brains of an ant, he'd have gone straight to Washington himself. And found out what I found out. But Stroud does things the rough way. Some fine morning he's going to gather those men who are camped outside town and move against Warbonnet. When our marshal gets here, there may be nothing for him to do but sift the ashes."

Madden said grimly, "Do you think I've waited five years to have Mace Stroud turn the trick I figure on turning?"

"You may not have a choice."

"Look," Madden said, "I know Stroud. He may go to bed every night with a big dream of knocking down Warbonnet's wire. But when he gets up in the morning and thinks about it, his bones turn to jelly."

"Don't be too sure," Luddington said. "I've learned a few things since I landed here. Warbonnet isn't as mighty as it was when you

41

left. My guess is that Ordway's a sick man; they say he hasn't showed himself off the ranch in a long time. His girl married an Eastern fellow, Rex Willard. Willard has got money — money enough to keep a gun crew in Warbonnet's bunkhouse, if needs be. But it takes more than guns and dollars to fight a war. When Stroud thinks of moving in on Warbonnet, he thinks of fighting Willard, not Ordway. It's made Stroud a bold man."

Madden shook his head. "I know Tucker Ordway. He couldn't get so sick that he couldn't run Mace Stroud down the road. Old Tuck's foxy. If he's lying low, it's a scheme to force Stroud into a move, and Warbonnet will be ready for it. I'll lay you ten to one that Stroud is afraid of just that."

Luddington sandpapered his huge jaw with his fingertips. "I wonder . . ." he mused aloud. "They say around town that several men in recent weeks have asked the way to Warbonnet. They haven't looked like gun-hands, but you never can tell. I've told you I've done some riding. There are guards at Warbonnet's gate. Maybe it will be a tough nut to crack, at that. And maybe you're right about Stroud."

Madden's jaw tightened. "The man who pulls Tucker Ordway down off his rawhide throne is going to be me, Ames!"

42

Luddington was silent for a long moment, and then he said slowly, "There's one thing you've never told me. Why do you hate Ordway so much?"

Madden, too, was silent. In the hallway a man lurched along, patently drunk; he found his room and did a great rattling with the key. A door slammed distantly; sound came from the street, and behind it was the far and rhythmic throbbing of the professor's piano in Pearl's Palace.

Then Madden said, "When I came to Frisco looking for a lawyer, there were plenty I could choose from. I'd heard that you were smart and ambitious and that when you put your teeth into something, all hell couldn't shake you loose. They said you had a ranch over in Nevada. Maybe that's just a plaything, but I figure it gives you some savvy of how horse-and-rope men think. That's why I hired you, but I told you only what you needed to know. That was then. You've proved that you're doing a good job. Now, take a look — "

He stood up from the chair and slowly unbuttoned his shirt and stripped it off. He stood naked from the waist up, and even in the dimness of this room, the skin of his chest and arms was startlingly white in contrast to the sun-darkened hue of his face. He had a good chest to him, and broad shoulders. He stepped toward the window and turned his back to Luddington.

Luddington looked and said hoarsely, "My God!"

Madden moved back to the chair and picked up the shirt and donned it. "A blacksnake made those scars," he said. "Tucker Ordway rode nowhere without that whip; he carried it for forty years. He made himself the law in the valley. Sometimes it was a good law. He kept men like Cibo Pearl from running crooked games and selling watered whiskey. He kept men like Mace Stroud from locating some poor devil on an alkali flat. He ran crooked gamblers out of town; he put the worst of the percentage girls on stagecoaches with one-way tickets. But when a man makes himself the law, he sometimes gets the notion he's God — sooner or later he throws one thunderbolt too many."

He was not a man given to long speeches, and he turned silent, his face grim with re-membering, then spoke again. "How would you like to be driven down yonder street with a man laying a blacksnake across your back? And you not able to lift a hand? What would you do, Ames, when you found yourself big enough to strike back?"

Luddington said, "I see . . . So you won't

44

rest till you pull him down, humiliate him in turn?"

"He had me pegged as a little man, not fit to step through the gate of Warbonnet. He'll live to learn that I'm bigger than he thought. The whipping is another matter. For that, he'll look at me through gunsmoke. And he'll be a ruined man that day, with only his gun left to him."

Luddington frowned thoughtfully. "I know two other men in this town who carry his whip-marks. They make no secret of it. Stroud and Pearl. When the game broke up tonight, I headed back here to find you. Stroud was ahead of me. I stood in the shadows and listened to what passed between you. Then it occurred to me that Pearl might come along, too, so I kept waiting. I saw what you did to him. That was a foolish play, Larry, and so was your turning down Stroud's offer. They want exactly what you want — Ordway humbled. You'd better make your peace with them."

"No," Madden said, the single word a small explosion of sound in the room. "Some things a man doesn't share. I've my way of doing business, and it isn't Stroud's or Cibo's. Get that straight, Ames!"

Luddington said, "What's next then?"

"We wait till your marshal gets here.

45

Meantime, we'll pretend to be strangers until the time comes to show our hand."

Luddington said slowly, "I think I shall like this job. I think I shall like it very much. But you're going to have to fight off Stroud and Pearl to get first crack at Ordway. It makes a queer sort of game."

"So be it," Madden said.

A cry lifted on the street, not made by some raucous cowboy liquored and feeling his oats; it had fear in it and shock and anger. Madden moved quickly to the window, and Luddington followed after him; they stood shoulder to shoulder, looking down. Lamplight splashed its saffron bars across the dust, and in this light and the stars', a wagon stood drawn up before the mercantile across the way. Around this wagon men were drawn, the babble of their voices lifting, their excitement a visible thing. Something dark and blanket-wrapped lay in the wagon bed, and as the two watched, ready hands lifted the object and carried it into the mercantile. Madden understood then. The mercantile was also the furniture store and stocked coffins.

"A dead man," Luddington said, not really interested.

"Yes," Madden said and guessed who it was, remembering that thunderous moment last night when he and Rex Willard had come

46

through a clump of trees to find three men awaiting them. There had been that one who'd lain still in the grass afterwards. Madden thought now to tell Luddington of this, but he was tired of talking; he wanted to be abed. So he held silent as the men below disappeared inside the mercantile and the crowd dispersed, still talking excitedly.

"A violent country," Luddington said, no shudder in his voice but only a mild astonishment, a mild speculation.

"I'll be getting to my room," Madden said. "I think I'll sleep the clock around."

He turned then and quitted the room, but he was still remembering that blanket-wrapped body; he was remembering that his own gun had taken the life from the man, and he was regretting it. Here, he reflected, was something more that could be traced to Tucker Ordway, if a man wanted to look at it that way. Violence was a rock dropped into water. There was a first ripple and the growing circles that spread from it. There was a beginning, but who could tell how far the ripples would reach?

4. Shadow of Evil

Warbonnet lay crowded up against the valley's western wall, a good twenty-five miles north of Sawtelle as the crow flies and near enough to Tumbling Wall that that great rock heap could be seen from Tucker Ordway's veranda at any hour save the darkest. Here, in this lifting end of the valley, there were timber for building and creeks that sparkled in the sun and good rich grass for summer pasture. Here was a cattleman's paradise, and Tucker Ordway had held it for half a century, a king who'd given scant regard to the pretentiousness of his palace; for the ranchhouse, low and long, was made of logs, sturdy against the storms but no kinder to the eye than it needed to be.

Bunkhouse and blacksmith shop and corrals and barn — all the strewn structures that made up the ranch headquarters — also showed the rough hand of Ordway, but the patio was of Willard's devising, his and Corinna's. Both had spent a season in southern California; and the patio, between ranchhouse and barn, had thus been inspired. War-bonnet's crew had obediently hauled any rock flat enough to pass for a flagstone and laid these in the hard earth; the huge fireplace was the product of Willard's own hands, for he had a rich man's pride in a manual skill that required mortar box and trowel. The table and wicker chairs Corinna had got from one of the mail order houses. A tinkling fountain made music all the day.

On this sunlit morning, they took a late breakfast in the patio, the two of them, Willard in his corduroy riding suit, Corinna in a print dress that made her look fragile and adolescent and altogether lovely. She was a fair-haired girl, unmarked by Montana's suns, and too often seemed mature beyond her years, for Warbonnet had that way of touching its own. Her eyes were as blue as Tucker Ordway's, but she was her deceased mother in all other ways, small-boned and oval-faced and given to quiet thinking and quiet judgments.

This morning, looking at her husband, she was troubled, feeling a need to talk but not wanting to alarm him with the run of her thoughts, so she said in her secret heart: *Please make him be careful! Make him be very careful!* for she was still thinking of his foot-sore return to the ranch the morning before;

she was thinking of that and his report of being harried by men and then rescued by one who hated him.

Willard smiled across the table. "How is your father this morning?"

Her eyes darkened. "I took him his breakfast hours ago. Why does he still get up at the crack of dawn when there's nothing for him to do? And then he sits all day, with that horrid whip on the floor beside him. Rex, wouldn't he be better if he could go away somewhere?"

Willard shook his head. "He'd never be happy off Warbonnet."

She shuddered. "I wish he'd let me destroy that painting. Every time I look at it and then look at him, I can see the changes the days are making. It's like watching a rock crumble away."

Willard reached across the table and took her hand in his. He had a gentleness to him and a quick understanding of all her moods. "You worry too much, dear."

"It's you I'm worried about mostly," she confessed. "When they've got so bold that they hunt you down with guns — !"

"It means nothing," he said. "They saw the shape of opportunity and intended only to have their fun. Then the chase got into their blood. I dare say they'll think twice the next time. They're good people, Corry. Stroud has got them to believing that Warbonnet is a fairy tale ogre."

"There's more to it than that, Rex. There's Larry."

Willard smiled. "If I'd lost you to him, I'd be crazy jealous, too."

Corinna said, "I never saw Larry after that horrible thing happened in town between him and Dad. But I know how terribly proud he is, and I know how that would have eaten into him. Yet he's a stranger now — a grim, terrible stranger, hating me and you and Dad and everything that is Warbonnet."

Willard said, "He's had his say to me. Maybe that got it out of his system. He's too big a man to be petty. I like to keep remembering that he saved my life."

Corinna had then a vision of a tall man riding, and with it came the milling memories, and she said, "Perhaps you're right. But I wish he'd ride on."

Willard said, "Hush! Somebody's coming," and lifted his hand for silence as Jess Barker rode around a corner of the ranch-house and stepped down from his saddle, looking scared. He made a contradictory figure, for his boots were stirrup-scarred and his sombrero was a cowboy's, but he wore the hated denim of the sodbusters. His deputy badge was a brightness upon his faded vest, but there was none of the law's dignity to him.

Willard rose and said, "Good morning," making it neither affable nor belligerent; and then, with a courtesy born of long habit: "Have you had breakfast?"

"No time for that," Barker said. "I rode most of the night."

Corinna rose, too, feeling fear, a new fear made of more than the intangibles that had troubled her this morning, feeling as though a cloud had passed before an uncertain sun and laid a black shadow upon her. She looked at Willard, worried for him; and Willard frowned, his eyes on Barker, and asked, "What brings you here?"

Barker moved his weight from one foot to the other and had the look of one with small taste for his duty. "You have some sort of ruckus with a few of the boys from town night before last?"

"No," said Willard and smiled. "They had some sort of ruckus with me."

"One of them's dead," Barker said.

Willard nodded. "That's why I'm alive."

Barker got it said then. "I've got to take you along."

"Take me along!"

"There's got to be some sort of coroner's inquest. You'll have to be a witness. What happens then depends on what the jury decides."

Willard turned to Corinna. "This shouldn't keep me in town long." He looked at Barker again. "I'll be ready in a few minutes," and he picked his hat from the flagstones beside his chair.

Corinna said, "No, Rex! Don't you see what they mean to do? It's a frame-up! They'll make a murder charge out of it."

"That's ridiculous," Willard said.

But her fear was a great, rushing thing, smothering her, smothering all the logic in her, and the signs of her fear were so visible that Willard said, "I want a word with my wife, Barker. Alone, if you don't mind."

Barker said, "Hell, I'm just doing my job," and turned and walked away from them.

Corinna said then, more calmly, "You don't have to go, Rex. The boys only let him through the gate because they knew we didn't have to let him out unless we wanted to. He's Mace Stroud's man — body and soul and badge. Once they have you in Sawtelle, they'll never let you leave. Don't you think Stroud's guessed by now that you're running Warbonnet?"

She was no gentle reed needing another's strength to sustain her, but she wanted his arms around her now; she wanted to feel his nearness and draw upon it. She leaned toward him, and his arms enfolded her, and his lips brushed her ear.

He said softly, "If Stroud is a betting man, he's betting that I won't dare come back with Barker. And that's how he hopes it will be. Can't you see that? Barker's the law — the only law in the Beavertail. Defy Barker, and we've given Stroud his excuse. We've outlawed Warbonnet then, and he can deputize all those land-hungry settlers and throw them against our wire."

She stepped back from him. "You're right, Rex," she said. "You'll have to do whatever you think best. I know that. But just the same, I'm scared — "

"Don't be," he said. "The inquest can only be a formality, once I confound them by showing up." He turned away from her and went to the corrals, and she watched as he did his own saddling. He was inept at it, but none of the lounging Warbonnet hands laughed, and none offered him help, and in those two things was the hallmark of their respect. Knowing this, Corinna had a surging pride in him, though the black shadow still touched her.

He skirted the patio with the saddled horse, lifting his hand to her. She waved back and forced herself to smile, and through her despair her pride loomed, strong and heady. She saw him ride away with Barker; she went to the ranchhouse gallery and watched until the two were lost to sight in timber that lay between the buildings and the far gate; and then she sat down, feeling suddenly sick at heart, feeling helpless.

All this had been so sudden that only her instinct had served her, but now she marshaled the facts, remembering each detail of what Rex had told her when he'd returned to the ranch the morning before. It came to her then: one man, and one only, could be the key to all that might happen at the inquest, and that man was Larry Madden, who'd fired the shot that had laid a man low. He'd fired in his own defense and in Rex's, and he could tell a jury so.

But afterwards he had told Rex that he hated him.

She came off the gallery then, stirred to action and glad for action, finding it an antidote for the dark thinking that disturbed her. She hurried toward the corrals and singled out one of the crew, a man grown gray in Warbonnet's service. He was Hap Sutton, foreman, and he'd known the trail north out of Texas with Tucker Ordway. To Sutton she spoke in low and urgent whispers while he listened, nodding sagely. . . .

Two things in all the valley might have startled a drifting rider to behold, for they were alien. One of them was the patio Rex Willard and Corinna had wrought; the other was the canopied bed of Cibo Pearl. But none save the elect had access to Pearl's quarters above his saloon, for here in an imported opulence he locked out the world. His room was garishly furnished and draped, and reeked constantly of perfume, and his bed was for the dreaming of a small-souled man whose courage had always fallen short of his dreaming.

On this morning when Jess Barker had dared to venture beyond Warbonnet's gate, Pearl lay in the canopied bed in a frilled nightgown, the fairy-tale toad in the royal chambers, a man petulant of face and sore of body; and he was thus when Reva entered. Seeing the breakfast tray he had ignored, she kept her smile inward and said in a calm voice, "The food didn't suit you?"

Pearl said, "He's lamed me for life; that's what he's done. Reva, when I kill him, I'm going to kill him slow, the way the Yaquis do."

Reva said, "I suppose you'd know about that. So it's Yaqui. I've always judged that you were part Indian, but I never knew which kind."

She was standing close enough to the bed so that he could reach and grasp her wrist, and he twisted it until pain stood in her eyes. "My dear, I am pure Castilian," he said. "That and English and high German and a few other breeds. But always I am Cibo Pearl. Do not forget that. And do not look for my roots in any other man, for Cibo Pearl is Cibo Pearl."

She wrenched free of him. "Mace Stroud is downstairs," she said. "He wants to see you."

He thought about this for a moment, his greasy moon-face screwed tight until his eyes were nearly lost in folds of flesh. "Send him up."

She left, her skirts making a soft swishing, and she ushered Stroud into the room within a few minutes. Stroud's huge, swinging arms at once imperiled bric-a-brac on tables and shelves. He came close to the bed and stood there, wrinkling his nose. "Gawd, it stinks in here!" he announced in his booming voice. He grinned at Pearl. "So you're lying low and licking your wounds, eh?"

Pearl's eyes hardened. "What is it you want, Mace?"

Stroud glanced at Reva, his face wary, but Pearl said, "You can talk before her. She belongs to Cibo Pearl."

Reva drifted to a chair by the window overlooking the street and seated herself, becoming unobtrusive. She showed them only half her face; her profile might have graced a

Greek coin. Stroud looked at her with a new speculation, the run of his thoughts showing, until Pearl said, "Well, Mace — ?"

"Heard about Madden bouncing you on the boardwalk," Stroud said. "There was some more excitement a little later. Some of my boys brought in a dead sodbuster. They'd been giving Willard a run, night before last, but Willard had met up with a man who could fight. The man was a stranger, but from the way the boys describe him, he was Larry Madden."

Pearl said, "*Madden* siding Rex Willard?"

"My guess is Madden was just riding in and ran into the ruckus. He'd be just the kind of damn' fool to take cards. It must have handed him a jolt when he found out who he was siding."

"And now — ?" Pearl asked thoughtfully.

"Now Jess Barker's out at Warbonnet asking Willard to come in for the inquest. We've scheduled it for tomorrow night."

Pearl frowned. "Willard's no such fool as that, Mace. Or if he is, Tuck Ordway will never let him set foot off Warbonnet."

"Naturally Willard's no such fool!" Stroud said impatiently. "But if he doesn't come, Jess will need about twenty more deputies to go after him. I can count on the settlers, but those plowboys won't stand up so tough against

58

Warbonnet guns. That's why I'm here. How many boys can you line up for me? I want the Peso Kid. You willing to loan him in the interests of law and order?"

Pearl thought about this. "It's a fool's play, Mace. Supposing Willard decides to come? And supposing Madden testifies that your men were crowding them when the shooting took place? How are you going to make a war against Ordway out of that?"

Stroud said, "If Madden testifies to save Willard's skin, I'll eat this damn' tent you've got over your bed. No, I'm not worrying about Larry. He wouldn't line up with me, but that doesn't mean he'll side Warbonnet. Remember, he's got whip-marks on his back, too."

"I don't like this scheme of yours," Pearl said. "It's got holes in it."

"I'll worry about that, Cibo. Do I get men from you?"

Pearl raised his eyes to Reva. "You've heard," he said. "Tell every man who draws my pay to ride if Mace wants him."

Reva nodded, and Stroud turned toward the door. "That's good enough," he boomed. "I'll show you how a man goes about stirring things up, Cibo. You never get anywhere lying in bed."

When the door had closed, Pearl sank back

59

against the pillows and gave himself to thinking, and then at long last he said, "Reva, find Peso and send him up here. I think, my dear, there's a way to plug one of those holes friend Mace has so carelessly left in his scheming."

She said, "You want Peso?"

His anger was like a volcano's, deep and sulphuric. "Isn't that what I said?"

Reva rose. "A man who plays with a loaded gun is bound to get into trouble. And Peso is a loaded gun."

"Send him up here!" he snapped.

"Very well," she said and quitted the room again, and shortly the Peso Kid stood in the doorway, slim and dark and deadly, the peso between his finger and thumb, the peso rising into the air to fall back to his hand.

Pearl said, "The eating good these days, Peso? And the drinking? And the girls?"

"*Si,*" said Peso.

"But a man grows tired of that, eh? A man wants to be doing the kind of work that he does well?"

"*Si, senor.*"

"There was one in the saloon last night, a tall one. He came to my table just before the game broke up. You remember him, Peso?"

The Kid nodded.

"Sometime before tomorrow night, Peso," Pearl said and cocked his thumb and extended

60

the index finger of his right hand, making a gun. "You savvy?"

"*Si!*" said the Peso Kid, and his dark eyes came alive then.

"Go, Peso."

And with the Peso Kid gone from the room, Cibo Pearl relaxed upon the pillows and considered the morning's work and found it good. He had served himself; he had served the cause to which he and Mace Stroud were tacitly pledged. He had done these two things in one fell stroke. True, there was the Yaqui way, and a man might have pleasured himself with considering it and thus eased the pain of his body. But expediency came first. And when your enemy died, that was the end of him and the end of it. This was the thought that kept Cibo Pearl smiling.

5. The Waiting Gun

True to his word, Madden slept the clock around and came again to Sawtelle's street in the drowsy afternoon. He had himself a haircut, a shave and a bath at the barber shop, then had a look in at the livery to see how his saddler was being treated. He took his supper in the hotel's dining room, and when the town began stirring to its night life, he sauntered into Pearl's Palace, wanting to show himself. If Cibo Pearl hungered for trouble after the incident of the night before, then Pearl could have his chance. But Pearl was nowhere to be seen. Ames Luddington was at poker with Mace Stroud and a couple of cowboys; the dark youth who employed himself at tossing a coin into the air stood against the bar. Reva was not around. Luddington gave Madden a nod, and Mace Stroud grinned wide, showing no malice for last night's rebuff. Madden nodded back and went outside.

Jess Barker came riding along the street with Rex Willard, but neither man saw Madden as he made an unobtrusive stand before the Palace. The pair rode past, and Madden's only thought was to wonder at Willard's temerity in riding back to a town where he had so recently found enemies, and from this came a grudging admiration for the Easterner. That Willard was in any sense a prisoner didn't strike Madden. Barker seemed half asleep in his saddle, and there was nothing of authority about him save his badge. The pair had the look of two who'd met on a trail and ridden in together.

So thinking, Madden walked to the Ogallala, climbed the stairs and let himself into his unlocked room and was instantly moving sidewards in the darkness, his hand dropping to his gun. Someone stirred in the room, and Madden was at once mindful of the enemies he had made, for he had not been reassured by Stroud's grin, and Pearl had carried a murderous anger away with him.

Then Reva's voice reached out, saying softly, "It's me."

Madden said, "I'll get the lamp burning."

"No!" she cried and moved toward him, coming close enough that her perfume was in his nostrils and he was suddenly conscious of her nearness and her femininity and conscious, too, of a lonely man's hunger. But he put no false estimate on her presence. Her kind never had to go seeking any man. So he

63

asked then, "What is it?"

"I've brought you a message," she said. "From Corinna Willard."

This surprised him, and his surprise must have manifested itself in his silence, for she said, "You find it hard to believe that I know Corinna? Is that it? You're thinking that Corinna would recognize me for what I am and not so much as speak to me. I ride often, Mr. Madden. Sometimes I've met Corinna on my rides. Perhaps she's as lonely as I am. Perhaps living in the shadow of Tucker Ordway has given her tolerance. We're friends, she and I."

"She came to town? To you?"

"She got word to me through Hap Sutton. She was afraid you wouldn't listen to any man riding a Warbonnet horse. She wants to see you, Madden. She wants you to ride to your old Circle M about noon tomorrow. Will you do that?"

His lips tightened. "Anything we had to say to each other was said long ago."

He could make out Reva in the darkness now; her shoulders lifted in a shrug. "I've delivered the message."

She moved toward the door, but at the threshold she paused, her face and shoulders glimmering whitely. "You don't want my advice, I know. But I hope you'll take it anyway.

Whether you go to see Corinna or not, I don't care. It might even be best if you didn't. Things dead are better left dead. But if you're wise, Madden, you'll ride out of here forever."

"Why?" he asked.

"Your hate has brought you back. Do you think anyone couldn't see that? You want Tucker Ordway's scalp, but you don't want it with the help of Stroud or Cibo. Oh, yes, I know of those things. Cibo talks to me as he'd talk to a horse, certain that I won't repeat what I hear. But no man ever got anything out of hate but bitterness in his mouth. That's why I advise you to ride out!"

He moved toward the doorway. "I'll see you back to the Palace."

She shuddered. "What do you suppose Cibo would do to me if he guessed that I'd come here?"

He made fists out of his hands, then let his fingers spread. "I hadn't thought about that," he said and stepped back from her.

She was gone then, and afterwards he stood in the room, not lighting the lamp, just thinking, thinking. . . . The piled-up heat of another day was here, and he had a wakefulness compounded from his long slumbering and from all the stirring memories the message from Corinna had brought him. He stood indecisively for many minutes, and then he went down to the street again and headed for the livery stable. Within fifteen minutes he was astride his horse and riding out of Sawtelle toward the north.

There had been a glimpsed figure loitering in the shadow of a cottonwood across from the livery, but he'd supposed it was some townsman taking the night air, or a cowboy needing a look at the stars after too much liquoring. . . .

With the night around him, Madden rode steadily to the north, but once he was beyond the tent town, he veered toward the eastern wall of the valley, thus riding wide of the maze of fences which now blocked this lower end of the Beavertail. Once beyond the homesteads, he turned northwest and let the miles drop behind as he angled across the valley's grassy middle, and in due course he was beneath the western hills. At long last he put his horse down a slope and came to the spot he sought. Here he offsaddled and spread the blanket and prepared to sleep. Now the darkness before dawn made a mystery of all the land, and it was not until the sunlight awoke him hours later that he looked upon that which he knew he would see.

Of the ranch buildings that had been his, only the stone chimney and fireplace of the house still stood, rearing gauntly amidst a jackstraw heap of charred beams. An iron bedstead that had withstood the fire sagged forlornly in the ruin, but what had been the barn was only a blackness upon the ground. When Madden had pulled on his boots, he sat cross-legged upon the blanket and had his look, remembering all of the pride that had once been his in this place. . . .

Lucky Larry they'd called the man who'd found so fine a piece of ground for himself.

There'd been cattle then, wearing his own Circle M brand, a herd carefully built across the seasons. If a man did all his own work, putting in as high as fifteen hours a day at it, burning up his youth and his energy and walking wide of the saloons, he sometimes piled up enough dollars in an old lard can to buy him another cow. That's the way he'd done it — the hard way. He remembered long hours in the saddle and himself heading here after dark, thinking of the supper he had to cook. Sometimes there'd been a broken fence on the way, and he'd fixed it by lantern light and afterwards tumbled into his bunk to remember sleepily that he'd forgotten to eat but being too tired to do anything about it.

Always there'd been another day, and another day's chores, but always, too, there'd been the big dream to spur him on. There was the neighbor to the north to remind him of the smallness of Circle M. And there was the girl who'd sometimes come riding and taken a precious hour out of his day, but he'd never counted the time lost, not when ambition's spurs were twice as sharp afterward. . . .

And so Madden reminisced through the morning until at last the sun stood high and he heard the jingle of a bit chain and turned for a quick look to the north, his wariness instinctive. Then he looked again toward the charred ruins and kept his eyes upon them until she dismounted beside his blanket and said softly, "Hello, Larry."

He arose and took off his sombrero and said, "Hello, Corinna."

These five years had matured her immeasurably; he saw that at once. In riding garb her body was rounded and youthful, and her face had all its old sweetness, but her eyes had lost their laughter. It shocked him to see her thus, freighted with worry, and pity moved him until he remembered Rex Willard.

She looked toward the ruins. "I've ridden here often," she said.

He made a slicing gesture with his hand. "I didn't mean there should be anything left for you to see."

"That was the cruelest thing of all," she said, not looking at him. "Your touching a match to it yourself."

"That was to save Tuck Ordway the trouble. It wasn't good enough ever — not near good enough."

She said, "Larry, that isn't fair. There was never a time when I wouldn't have married you and come here to live. You know that. I told you so time and again. It was your own stiff-backed pride that made you dream a foolish dream like building a place as big as Warbonnet before you brought me to it. Oh, Larry, you threw away your own chance!"

He said, "It worked out well for you. You sold yourself to a lot higher bidder."

That brought her head up; she looked as though he'd struck her with a whip. "It's true, Larry, that I married Rex because he had more money than any other man who paid attention to me back East. But that was three years after you'd left."

He said, "The only word I ever got was from a drifter I met in Tucson. He'd worked for Hashknife for a spell. He said you'd married some moneybag named Rex Willard. I was shooting in the dark just now. I seem to have hit."

Her shoulders sagged and she said in a small voice, "Tucker Ordway wanted a son — someone to take over Warbonnet when his day was done. I grew up knowing that every time he looked at me he was remembering that I had cost him the life of his wife and that when he died, Warbonnet died with him. Well, I brought him a son after all. One with the money to bolster Warbonnet now that the wolves are yapping at its gate. Was it a completely wicked thing I did, Larry?"

Her sincerity took the belligerency out of him. "I don't know," he said. "I don't know."

"I didn't come here to turn a knife in you, Larry."

"Why did you come?"

"To ask you what you're going to do at the inquest."

"Inquest — ?"

"You didn't know? The inquest for that man who got killed a couple of nights ago when you helped Rex outrun those settlers."

He recalled Willard's riding into town with Jess Barker then, and he understood. *The fool!* he thought.

"If I know Mace Stroud," Corinna said, "he'll make a murder charge out of it. That coroner's jury will be hand-picked. What are you going to do about it, Larry?"

"Do?" he asked and his old resentment burned brightly again. "Why should I do anything?"

Her voice dropped lower. "I've told you why I married him. There were other reasons besides. He is a good man — a kind man. Is it possible that a wife could fall in love with her husband? I love him, Larry."

He began to laugh then, but there was little humor in it. "I fished him out of the fire once. Now I'm to go on fishing him out. Is that it?"

She said dismally, "I can't make you do anything, Larry. There just wasn't anybody else I could turn to."

He looked at her and saw now the full measure of her fear and her grief, and he passed his hand before his eyes and was suddenly a man confused. He had lived a long time with his hate, so long that sometimes he had grown tired of it, feeling less free than when Circle M had claimed him and ambition had burned with a clearer flame. Now he said, "Willard — old Tuck — Warbonnet — you. Each is part of the other, and I don't know where the hate leaves off."

She gestured toward the charred ruins. "I would have lived there once. You know that. I think, Larry, that you owe me something."

He wondered then if any man could be a match for a woman, for he knew himself beaten and found the knowledge less bitter than he'd supposed. Her defenselessness had made him defenseless. He lifted his hands to her shoulders. "Ride back to Warbonnet," he said. "I'll be heading south. To testify that I handled the gun in self-defense."

She began to cry softly, and he turned her around and headed her toward her horse. "Get going," he said gruffly. "We're burning daylight now."

Obediently she climbed into the saddle; she sat looking down at him and said, "Thank you, Larry," and rode away then. Afterwards he caught up his own hobbled horse and freed the animal and swung blanket and saddle to its back. But when he was ready to ride, he sat his saddle for one last look at the old place, and looking, he had to laugh again, remembering all the hours and the toil and the poverty, thinking of the irony of that when he considered what had happened afterwards.

For he had ridden away with the smoke rising to the sky, and he'd had no goal, not caring where his trail took him. There'd been that ranch in Nevada, and he'd lasted until the foreman, finding him cooling himself in a waterhole, had showed curiosity about the scars on his back, and he'd laid his fist on the foreman in a sudden, seething anger. After that there'd been Colorado and New Mexico and Arizona, and he'd drunk more than was good for him, and his horse and saddle had crossed a poker table. That was how he'd come to go prospecting, and the gods had had their laugh when a cowpoke, covering the trails of the grizzled men of the mountains, had stumbled upon the lode they'd long overlooked. And thus in a single day he'd turned richer than a thousand years of toil on this Circle M might have made him.

That was when he'd emptied his last bottle, for suddenly there'd been something to live for, now that he'd had the means to make it possible. Overnight he'd become big enough to pit himself against Tucker Ordway, and he'd faced northward again, but first he'd employed Ames Luddington, for he'd needed Luddington's kind of savvy for the fight he'd intended to make.

That was how it had been, but now he sat his horse with a need to be moving and that need arose from the greater need of Rex Willard of Warbonnet. He remembered Reva urging him to ride on, and he wondered how much she had guessed of what Corinna's request would be.

But he had passed his word, and he put his horse up the slope, climbing toward a clump of trees at its crest, and he was nearly into those trees when the gun spoke. He felt the shock of the bullet along his ribs, and the force of it lifted him from his saddle and flung him to the ground; pain came in surging waves, bringing nausea, bringing oblivion.

He heard a soft voice from afar, yet the

words were clear in his consciousness. He heard a man say, "In the darkness I lose you; in the daylight I find you. It is good, *senor.*"

He tried to look upward, knowing that a man towered above him. It might have been any man, save that this one held a smoking gun in his right hand while his left played with a coin, tossing it into the air and letting the sunlight dance upon it, catching it deftly as it came down.

6. At Summit House

He lay in a troubled darkness and fought against that darkness, dimly conscious of sound and movement around him, conscious of pain. Time had no meaning for him. He'd heard shots after he'd fallen, but that might have been an hour ago or a day ago; perhaps it was the shots that reached through oblivion and brought him this half-awareness that was like being blind. He wanted nothing more than to sink back into the pit, away from his agony, away from all the confusion. He felt hands tugging at him, and he supposed they were the hands of that lean, deadly one who flipped the coin. He tried to strike out; he willed himself to do this and made a feeble flailing with his arms.

A voice got through to him saying, "Try to stand," but it wasn't a man's voice. That was the surprising thing. The voice was urgent and the tugging hands were urgent; he recognized the voice, but he couldn't tie a name to it. Not at first. Then it came to him that it was Reva's, but this made no sense. Reva was supposed to be in Sawtelle, at Pearl's Palace.

She was saying, "I've got to get you on your horse!" and he tried standing then and finally made it. His left side was soggy, and the pain dwelt there. He opened his eyes and had a blurred impression of land and sky and saw Reva looking scared. He said, "It's you all right," and felt comforted. The sun hurt his eyes, and he closed them quickly, but he'd located his horse, and he lurched toward it. He came against the horse and clutched at its solidness, finding the mane and twining his fingers in it. He put his weight against the horse and hoped the mount wouldn't move off.

Reva was working with his right hand, guiding it, and he felt the saddlehorn beneath his fingers. She said, "You've got to try to mount!" and he instinctively crooked his left leg and fumbled until she steered his boot into the stirrup. Raising himself was the hardest part of all; and when he did swing into the leather, he was afraid he'd tumble off the other side. He clutched the saddlehorn grimly with both hands.

Reva said, "Just hang on. I'll lead you."

He was glad not to have to put thought to what he was doing. He hung on, and presently he was moving; he risked opening his eyes again and saw that Reva was mounted, too, and was trailing his horse behind her own. He saw the western hills lifting above him; to his right was the sweep of the slope overlooking Circle M. The world seemed to undulate, land and sky blurring together and making him dizzy. He closed his eyes again.

He had the sensation that they were climbing; presently the smell of pine was strong, and the sun no longer blazed at him when he ventured a look; the sun was lost in a tangle of tree tops. They rode onward, and he had moments of clarity and moments of confusion; then he fell from the horse.

He had no remembrance of falling; his first awareness was that he was on the ground again and Reva was hovering over him, her voice frantic. After that, he went through the ordeal of mounting once more. They rode onward.

After a long while, Reva said, "You may climb down now."

He opened his eyes to find himself in a stump-dotted clearing before a large, two-story log house. He remembered this place, but he couldn't put a name to it, any more than he had been able to tie anything to Reva's voice when he'd first heard it. He knew that he should know all about this building, but he wasn't sure where it was or what purpose it served, and thinking was too much effort. He started to dismount, and the ground rushed up to meet him; blackness came again, and he fell deep into its feathery depths and heard Reva's voice, incoherent and far away, like the ghost of a voice.

When he came again to consciousness, he looked overhead and saw a beamed ceiling and realized that he lay upon a plank floor inside the building they had reached. The smell of dust was here and all the stored-up odors of antiquity. His head was pillowed on a slicker; when he tried lifting his head, Reva moved at once into his range of vision. She was wearing a divided riding skirt and a matching jacket heavily brocaded with silver.

She asked, "How do you feel?"

"I'll live," he told her and managed to grin.

He had another look around and saw a bar running the length of the room, a dusty bar, cobweb-festooned. A few crippled tables and chairs were scattered about the place. "Summit House," he said, for he remembered now. Once a stage road had climbed these western hills rimming the Beavertail and dropped down the slope to snake on to Sawtelle. This place had been a way station, where horses were changed and the passengers could put up for the night. He'd been in this building in the old days; there was this huge barroom on the ground floor and rooms upstairs.

Reva knelt down on the floor beside him, looking at him in a worried and searching way. "I couldn't drag you any farther. You're quite a load, and you weren't much help. But I did manage to get you bandaged."

His fingers explored and found the cloth against his ribs. It was, he judged, her petticoat. He asked, "How deep did he nick me?"

"He just grooved the flesh over your ribs. Pain and shock must have knocked you out then. You've lost blood; that's why you've kept fainting. I cleaned you up. There's a well out back. Would you like a drink?"

"Where did you learn a sawbone's trade?"

She said in a thin voice, "Do you think I've worked in a dozen honkytonks without learning how to care for a gunshot wound? You're not the first man I've doctored."

He could think clearly now. "You knew about that kill-crazy kid? You followed him?"

She shook her head. "I think that Peso took your trail last night. I must have been hours behind him. I came to Circle M to see whether you met Corinna or not. Call it a woman's curiosity, if you like. I saw the Kid waiting and understood why he was waiting; Cibo sent for the Kid yesterday morning. I was in a grove of trees up the slope, hiding where I could watch you and Corinna. When the Kid dropped you from your horse, I cut loose with a saddle gun. The Kid must have thought I was someone from Warbonnet. He turned and made fast tracks."

Madden said, "Do you suppose he turned back again?" and he was remembering her fear of Pearl and what might come of Pearl's knowing her part in all this.

She shook her head. "I watched him till he was out of sight. The Kid probably figured you were dead when you went down. He's not used to missing."

"But Cibo will be wondering what's keeping you."

Again she shook her head. "This is my day off. I usually ride when I'm free. That's how I first met Corinna, remember."

Madden said, "Cibo wasted no time at evening things up," and then, suddenly, he saw the real reason why the Kid had come gunning. "That inquest? When is it?"

"Tonight," Reva said.

He raised himself up then; he was weak as a kitten, but he got to a tottering stand and took a step toward the open door, the ancient floor squealing beneath him. He saw that the pines fringing the clearing laid long shadows; the sun was lost to his sight in the upper timber and its last goldenness was surrendering to the night. He turned to Reva and asked desperately, "Where did you put the horses? I've got to get to town. Don't you see? Cibo wanted to make sure I didn't testify tonight."

She said, "I thought to take you to town. That would have been too dangerous. I could have headed north to Warbonnet, but you wouldn't have thanked me for putting you in Tucker Ordway's care. Then I remembered this place. I wanted a roof over you in case you had to be left. But it's all of twenty miles to Sawtelle. You'd never make it in time."

Her calmness, her logic reached out to him, quieting his urgency, but he could still feel the pull of it. "I've got to try," he said.

She shrugged. She left the place and disappeared around its corner; he watched her until she was gone from sight, liking that smooth way she walked. He remembered then that there'd been a stable behind Summit House. He stood waiting for her, missing her at once. The place seemed deathly quiet without her; somewhere in the upper reaches of this rotting old pile, a rat scurried. Reva came back leading his horse and her own, and she stood by until he was into his saddle. He found that he didn't need to clutch the horn. When she'd mounted, he looked at her and said, "You can't go into town with me."

"I can ride along until you're almost there.

It will be deep dark then."

He nodded, not wanting to argue this; and she led the way into the timber and found the old stage road and began following it downward. Time had nearly obliterated the road; grass grew now between ruts that were mere shadows, sometimes lost. They walked the mounts, Madden fighting his impatience, and before they had cleared the timber, darkness enfolded the Beavertail and they had to grope along. Presently the moon rose; they reached the levels, but the land lay broken by coulees and ridges, shadows against silver, and their pace stayed slow. Beyond this country, they made better time, crossing the flatness of the valley's broad floor. But trotting awoke the pain in Madden, and he knew that Reva had been right; he could never make it to Sawtelle in time.

He gave up thinking about this, except with a corner of his mind; his word could still be the saving of Willard, inquest or no inquest, and his destination was still Sawtelle. They came into the cluttered homesteads as the moon rode high. Reva knew her way among these, and he was grateful for her knowledge; she found the gates and led him on a zig-zag course that skirted plowed fields and much wire. Sometimes light showed in a shack and the barking of a dog made a frenzy of sound in the night; once they heard the steady beat of an axe as a farmer worked late at his kindling. Reva avoided the shacks, and Madden understood why. There must be no man to tell with whom she had ridden this night.

Then, with the lights of Sawtelle before them, she drew rein and said, "I leave you here."

It was past midnight, he knew, and whatever a coroner's jury had found for Rex Willard was long since over and done with. The minutes no longer counted, and having them to spare, he drew rein likewise, and he said, "I owe you my life. I know that. Is there anything I can do for you?"

She thought about this, her face a study in the moonlight, her face extremely grave. She said, "I gave you a piece of advice. I told you to ride out. Will you do that, once you've had your say for Willard?"

He shook his head. "You haven't given me a good reason to go with it."

"I saw your back today when I bandaged you. I saw the whip-marks. If you stay, Tucker Ordway dies. Is that it?"

His lips tightened. "If I'd been put to picking the one woman in the world who might have understood, I'd have picked you."

She said, "I've never laid eyes on Tucker Ordway in my life. I've been here only a year, you know. Still, he's the best friend I ever had."

His eyebrows lifted. "You'll have to come again on that one!"

She said, "Drift from one town to another as I have, and you'll find them all cut from the same pattern. Cattlemen come in and throw their herds upon the hills and then a town springs up and perhaps a railroad comes. But the towns are made up of good people and bad — the merchants who hope to earn a dollar off cattleman trade, the bloodsuckers like Cibo who figure that a cowboy's coin is legitimate loot. You have churches and box socials and civic improvement meetings, but you also have fixed wheels and marked cards and watered whiskey. And girls like me. And you have men like the Peso Kid hanging off in the shadows, seeing to it that nobody breaks up the play of the Cibo Pearls. Do you follow me?"

He said grimly, "I'm ahead of you. What you're saying is that there comes a need for law. But that gives one man the right to swing a whip and call himself the law?"

"Necessity gives him the right! The Pearls and the Strouds and the Peso Kids would have swallowed Sawtelle whole long ago if it hadn't been for Tucker Ordway. Perhaps he made a mistake when he laid his whip to you;

I think I know why he did it. But when you call him to account, he'll go down in the dust, or you will. Who wins then? If you die, you're dead. If you live, then Sawtelle has lost the only law it's had."

"There's Yellow Lodge," he said.

"With a sheriff who's so unconcerned with Sawtelle that he appoints someone like Jess Barker? Yellow Lodge is sixty miles away."

He looked down at his hand, making a fist of it, then opening it. "You're trying to tell me I'm selfish."

She said, "You asked me what you could do for me. I've told you." She extended her hand. "Good night."

He said, "You forgot to weigh one thing into it: a man's pride." He took her hand and found the pressure of her fingers firm. He touched the brim of his sombrero. "Good night, Reva," he said.

He wheeled his horse and rode away from her; he came into Sawtelle's street and found Pearl's Palace still blazing with light, still raucous. A couple of the other saloons were open as well, but most of the town lay wrapped in darkness, and at the livery stable end of the street the shadows lay deep and the breeze rustled the leaves of the cottonwoods.

Madden aroused the hostler and had his horse put up. He said pointedly to the hostler,

85

"So you had yourselves an inquest tonight."

The hostler stood staring at him, and he realized then what a spectacle he must make, his shirt in ribbons, showing that crude bandage with the bloodstain on it. But his mood was both reckless and impatient and tinged with a faint anger that had been with him since his last words with Reva. Some of his petulance must have shown in his face, for the hostler took a careful step back from him and said, "The inquest was early in the evening."

Madden said, "Will you spit it out, man? What was their verdict?"

"Murder," the man said. "They'll have to move Willard to the county seat for trial."

Madden walked from the stable and stood at the edge of the boardwalk long enough to fashion a quirly. He drew deep upon the tobacco and did his thinking, and he knew then that there was no more to be done, not tonight. He was hungry, and he needed sleep; he could feel the toll of his wound and that long ride down from the hills. Tomorrow he would talk with Ames Luddington.

7. Cross-Purposes

He slept fitfully, favoring his wounded side; and when he roused, it was mid-morning and the sun was making itself felt in the hotel room. At first he lay in bed, taking his own time at coming to full wakefulness, but soon he got up and washed and shaved and found then that his step was steady. He went along the hall to Luddington's room, but the lawyer was not in. He went down to the dining room and ate and came out to the street. He crossed over to the mercantile and bought himself a new shirt, turning a bleak face to the curious stares of bonneted shoppers and the few loafers along the boardwalk.

Reva's bandage still held, but Madden asked the way to a doctor's and was directed to one whose place was at the end of the street. This medico kept his office in his home; he was a brusque graybeard whose face was familiar to Madden. He had a look at the wound, silently swabbed it with iodine and placed a new bandage upon it. These minis-trations finished, Madden donned the shirt he had purchased.

"Well — ?" Madden asked.

"Was a day," said the doctor, "when anybody old enough to call himself a man would have spit tobacco juice into a scratch like that and gone about his business. Just be careful you don't bust it open and you'll be fine in a few days."

The medico picked up the petticoat bandage and was about to carry it from his office when Madden glanced toward the strip of cloth and said, "That might have belonged to anybody, eh, Doc? Just anybody."

The medico said, "Do you think I'd have lived long enough to have gray whiskers if I hadn't learned never to talk about the things I see?"

Madden's grin was cold. "And that goes for the whip-marks on my back?"

"It doesn't keep me from thinking. I remember you now. You're Madden, who had that place south of Warbonnet. And I can tell what brought you back; it shows in your eyes. Forget it, son. It will be a sorry day for you if you don't."

Madden's lips thinned down, and he laid two silver dollars on the doctor's desk. "It wasn't advice that I came for."

"No," said the doctor and looked old. "It never is. It never is."

In the sunlight again, Madden stood for an aimless minute; there were several things he must do, and one of them was to find Luddington, and another was to see Willard, but suddenly there was a need more important than either of these, and he went resolutely to Pearl's Palace and barged in through the batwings. The saloon was nearly deserted at this nooning hour; a solitary barkeep lazed behind the mahogany, the swamper was still listlessly at work, and chairs were piled upon all the tables save one. Here a couple of townsmen dawdled at cards. Madden crossed directly to the bar. "Where," he asked, "will I find that half-pint Mexican who spends his spare time flipping a coin?"

"Peso? He ain't showed around yet today."

"And Cibo — ?"

The barkeep's eyes moved to the stairs at the rear of the room — the stairs leading upward to Pearl's quarters. "The boss has been keeping to bed. You know why, I guess."

"You can tell him," said Madden, "to move over and make room for his friend Peso. Will you remember that?"

The barkeep's face turned wooden. "I'll tell him."

Madden took a quick look around. He'd thought that Luddington might be here, but perhaps the lawyer had gone riding. He'd thought, too, that he might find Reva in the place, but it had been a hard night for Reva and he supposed she was still in bed.

But mostly he'd wanted to see the eyes of the Peso Kid when the Kid first found him still alive. He had a score to settle with Peso, and anger beat in his temples as he left the saloon. He searched this anger and found that it stemmed from what the doctor had said, which in turn had been a vague echo of Reva's words last night. A man got tired of meeting people who knew his business better than he knew it himself! Thus he'd wanted the Peso Kid so he could vent his futile fury. Realizing this, he felt like one caught in a childish act; and his anger ebbed then, leaving only a resolution with no great urgency to it. He would deal with the Kid when the time came.

He cut across the dust to the jail, a frame structure, false-fronted and distinguishable only by its barred windows. To the front of the building was Jess Barker's office, but the deputy was not in when Madden entered. Here stood a littered desk, a swivel chair and a pot-bellied stove, unused at this season and crammed to overflowing now with discarded papers. Behind the desk was a door giving into a corridor flanked by two cells on either side. Only one of these was occupied, and when Madden called, "Willard — ?" the man rose from a cot and came to the barred door.

Madden said, "So you walked right into it."

"Oh, it's you," Willard said, showing no surprise nor gladness nor antipathy, showing nothing. He had a day's stubble on his face and his corduroy riding suit looked as though he'd slept in it.

Madden said, "I hear they threw the book at you."

Color stained Willard's sallowness. "Isn't that what you expected?"

"Look," Madden said, "the only reason I wasn't here was because they saw to it that I couldn't be."

Willard thought about this, and then he said, "I'm sorry. But what would *you* have been thinking if you'd stood alone last night?"

Madden made a motion with his hand, banishing this kind of talk. "How did it go?"

"It was an interesting farce," Willard said. "They didn't waste much time at it. The coroner is a medico. He testified that the fellow had died from a gunshot wound. He'd dug out the bullet. Looked like a thirty-eight, he claimed. I carry a thirty-eight, and this is a country where everybody else carries a forty-five. The two main witnesses were those other two we met by the trees — the one you knocked from his horse and the one who rode away. They lied clumsily and didn't seem to

91

have much heart for it, but they lied just the same. They swore that no gun was lifted from leather but mine."

Madden frowned. "They admit they'd been trying to run you down?"

Willard shook his head. "Their story was that they'd been taking a ride to look for land they might file on. They'd met me, and I'd ordered them out of that end of the valley, claiming they were too close to Warbonnet's wire. One word had led to another, and I'd reached for my gun."

"And when you testified that you hadn't, that I'd done the shooting, what then?"

Willard said, "You weren't mentioned. Either by them or by me."

"What's that?" Madden demanded.

"You weren't mentioned."

"That just doesn't make sense!"

Willard shrugged. "I was the one they wanted framed, so they weren't playing up any second party. So I left you out of it, too. You saved my life that night. What kind of gratitude would it have been to point my finger at you to save my own skin?"

Madden reached for his tobacco and shaped up a quirly, taking a long time at this. He got the smoke going. Then he said, "You damn' fool! You crazy damn' fool!"

"The verdict was death from a gunshot

wound inflicted by me. I'm to be taken to Yellow Lodge and tried for murder. It's a county affair now, you see."

Madden said. "Tell me this: how long will it be before Tuck Ordway rides in with Warbonnet's crew and tears this shebang off you?"

Willard's face stiffened. "That won't happen."

Madden let smoke sift through his nostrils while he turned this over carefully in his mind. "Then I'm going to have to believe that Ordway's dead."

"No," Willard said. "But Corry will know that I wouldn't want to be snatched from jail. Turn outlaw, and I've played into Stroud's hands. I've still got a chance — a good chance. They won't run the court at Yellow Lodge."

Madden dropped his cigarette to the floor and ground it beneath his heel. "It won't come to that. They'll hold their stinking inquest over again when I get through talking to the coroner. Who is he? That whiskered old-timer?"

"No, that's Dr. Stone. Do you think they'd have been able to stage their farce last night if they didn't own the coroner body and soul? His name's Medwick, and he's new here since your time. If you want to help me, you'll have

93

to do your helping at Yellow Lodge."

"We'll see," Madden said and tramped out through Barker's office to the street.

The first man he stopped told him that Medwick had no office but kept quarters above the mercantile building. Madden climbed a covered stairway to the coroner's door and pounded upon it, getting no answer. He put his hand to the door; it gave to his touch, letting him into a littered kitchen where flies made a great buzzing. Silence was here, broken only by this droning, and snores which came from an adjacent room. The smell of whiskey hit Madden, and he had only to follow his nose to find Medwick's bedroom, where the man lay asleep in a tangle of blankets. Upon the floor was an empty whiskey bottle.

Madden shook the man, but Medwick only rolled over, clutching at the blankets with an intent mindlessness. He had rolled into bed fully clothed, and only one of his shoes was on the floor. Again Madden shook the man, calling his name loudly and putting a fierce violence into his hands. Medwick mumbled and opened his eyes for a moment, but there was no sense in them.

Madden looked down upon this sodden mass of a man, knowing now that he could do nothing with him, and his anger rose. He picked the whiskey bottle from the floor and hurled it through the window. As the glass shattered, he turned to the door. He came down the covered stairway to encounter Corinna upon the street.

She had just ridden in. He was sure of that, for the dust of travel lay upon her, but it was her eyes that held his attention; her eyes were frightened.

She said, "Larry!" and looked as though she might fall.

He put a hand to her arm, and he said, "I'll tell it quickly. I didn't get back to town yesterday; they fixed that. They've hung a murder charge on him and he goes to Yellow Lodge. But I'll be there. You can bet your last dollar I'll be there."

She took the news better than he'd hoped; she was Tucker Ordway's daughter. She looked as desperate as before, and her face was drawn, but she had hold of herself now. She said, "And I'll be there, too. When they move him, I'll go along."

Madden said, "Go down to the jail now and see him. That will be better than anything else today brings him."

She nodded, and he had the feeling that his words had got to her only as they'd got to Medwick, in a haze, through which they scarcely registered. She turned and walked away, and he watched her go; he watched until she stepped into Barker's office. Then he went back to the Ogallala House and climbed the creaky stairs, heading for his own room; but on second thought he moved on to Luddington's and raised his knuckles to the door. Luddington's voice bade him enter.

Madden stepped inside and said, "I've been looking for you."

"And I've been looking for you," Luddington said. He had stripped off his coat and was seated on the edge of his bed, his briefcase open and papers strewed over the blanket. "You weren't in your room at midnight, so I went riding around."

"Looking for me in the dark?"

Luddington shrugged. "You had me worried."

"I hired you as a lawyer," Madden said, "not as a nursemaid."

Luddington's strong face stiffened. "You're not talking to Mace Stroud now, Larry. Nor to Cibo Pearl."

Madden made a movement with his hand. "I'm touchy today, Ames." He sat down. "Did you miss the inquest?"

"No, that was early in the evening. It was quite a performance, from a lawyer's viewpoint. Justice *a la* Sawtelle." He smiled, making a show of his teeth.

96

Madden said, "I'm glad you were there." He turned the chair around and straddled it. "When they move Willard to Yellow Lodge, you're going to defend him."

Luddington frowned. "How's that?"

"You're going to defend him, because I'm the man who knocked that fellow out of his saddle, Ames."

He told all of it then, his riding down off the Wall and finding Willard harried and helping the man. And while he talked, Luddington sat thoughtful, his frown deepening.

"Self-defense," Luddington said at the end of it. "We could make fools of all of them five minutes after I put you on the stand. But why, Larry? Why this for Willard?"

There was this yet to be told to Luddington: how Corinna had sent for Madden and what she'd said to him and what had happened afterwards, after he'd given his promise to her. But this was something that belonged only to Madden, so he made his answer brief. "Because I want it that way."

Luddington said slowly, "I've begun to see the picture here. Warbonnet isn't Tuck Ordway any more; it's Rex Willard. He's young, and he's an idealistic fool. Otherwise he'd have told the whole truth at the inquest. Knock down Willard and we've as good as knocked down Warbonnet's wire. It's Tucker

Ordway you want, isn't it? Then let them haul Willard from Yellow Lodge's courthouse to the gallows or the penitentiary."

Madden shook his head. "We're just not playing it that way."

Luddington said, with a show of heat, "Damn it, Larry, your notion violates all common sense! I won't defend him!"

Madden stood up. "You've quit being my lawyer, is that it, Ames?"

It came to him that he'd been at cross-purposes with too many men today — the doctor, and Willard with his notions of standing trial, and the coroner, who had been so stupidly drunk. Luddington made just one too many. He met Luddington's eyes and held them. He saw then the strength of Luddington and the hardness, and he wondered how it would be to have Luddington pitted against him. He held Luddington's eyes for a long moment, but there was no reading the man, Luddington had played too much poker for that.

Then, at long last, Luddington shrugged. "Have it your way, Larry. You're footing the bills. But I've got to warn you that you're defeating yourself."

"We'll see," Madden said and left the room.

8. The Stranger

At lamplighting time Cibo Pearl paced his quarters above the Palace, still limping slightly, and about him there was a mountain cat's restlessness and sharp wariness. He had dressed in his customary black, but as yet he had not showed himself downstairs; his supper had been brought to him, but again the tray stood scarcely touched. He had kept the room dark; in the faint glow that came through the window, he made a black ungainly blob, moving always to and fro.

When the knock came at the door, he started; then remembering, he said, "Come in."

Mace Stroud stepped inside, bringing with him through the opened doorway the sounds of the barroom below, the voices and the scuffling of feet, the tinkling of glasses and the monotonous beat of the professor's piano.

Pearl said, "Shut that door, Mace."

Stroud obeyed, then moved ponderously forward, his huge hands out. "Show a light before I fall over something and break my neck!"

"I want to watch the street," Pearl said. "It is better this way. There is a chair to your left."

Stroud groped to the chair and put his weight down into it, sighing the pleasured sigh of a big man relaxed. "By thunder, I don't know how you stand the smell of this place, Cibo. What kind of man are you to keep yourself soaked in that stink-water?"

Pearl said softly, "Some day you are going to complain about a man's personal habits and find that he resents it, Mace."

"Every man to his own notions," Stroud said and waved a hand. "Sit down, Cibo. You'll wear out your fancy rug."

Pearl said, "Will you tell me what is keeping that damned stagecoach?"

"You're mighty jumpy tonight. Was there a time the coach ever got here short of a half hour late? Keep your britches on. Everything's going fine."

Pearl fished out his watch and snapped open the case and moved to the window to get light enough for a look. "Mace, something is wrong! Ordway must know by now. Why hasn't he hit at the jail?"

Stroud shrugged. "Our good luck."

"His girl — is she still in town?"

"She was, up to half an hour ago. She spent most of the afternoon in the jail-house, mooning with Willard through the bars. She took supper at the Ogallala. Figure it for yourself, Cibo. It was just last night we hung the deal on Willard. The girl shows up today, but I've seen no other Warbonnet saddler in town. Probably Tuck's waiting for her to fetch back the news. She's stayed in town instead. So that leaves Warbonnet waiting."

Pearl shook his head. "The tiger changes his stripes? Since when has Tucker Ordway taken to waiting for someone to come along to tell him what to do?"

Stroud said again, "Our good luck."

Pearl still stood by the window. Heat lay in the room, heat and the heavy reek of perfume; the dark drapery made of this a smothered place. Pearl said, "There goes Peso now, riding out. He rides alone."

Stroud said, "I told them to drift out one by one, or two by two. I don't want anybody noticing and then adding it up afterwards."

Pearl kept his attention on the street below. "He moves like a cat in the night," he said, half to himself. "I wonder . . . He might get into Warbonnet's house and out again with that picture. He has the nerve for the job, but has he got the brains? I have never offered him a price. . . ."

Stroud snorted. "You must dream about

that damn' picture! When I spit in Tuck Ordway's eye, I want the man, not his picture."

"Hit a man's dignity, Mace, and you have hurt him the hardest." He took his eyes from the street. "How many are you sending?"

Stroud counted on his fingers. "Six — maybe seven. Gunther's wife's ailing and he didn't know whether he should leave. But he's a cousin to what's-his-name. The fellow Madden shot. I think he'll ride."

Pearl said, "But will those settlers go through with it? When they chased Willard that night, they had their tempers up, but this is another matter. Will their stomachs turn when it comes to doing what they've got to do?"

Stroud said wonderingly, "By thunder, you *are* jumpy! Why do you suppose I'm having Peso head 'em? Peso will do what needs to be done. Just having the rest of them there will make them part of it. Whoever heard of a one-man lynching bee?"

"You felt out their tempers?"

"They've been muttering ever since last night. I gave them a good talk. 'Look,' I said, 'do you want Willard turned loose by some slick-talking Yellow Lodge lawyer?' A couple of them were in favor of kicking in Jess Barker's door right then and dragging Willard out. Then I had to talk them out of that.

'Look,' I said, 'what about the boys around town who ride for Hashknife and Rocker-S and T-Square? You want to make a rancher-homesteader war out of it?' It took tall talking, but I put it across that my way is simpler and safer."

Someone knocked at the door, and again Pearl started. He crossed the room and opened the door a few inches, and then he said, "Oh, it's you!" One of the barkeeps stood silhouetted by the light of a lamp posted at the head of the stairs. He gestured toward the supper tray, and Pearl said, "You can take it away." The man moved toward the canopied bed, leaving the door open behind him. Again sound seeped into the room; two men made boisterous argument at the bar below, their words incoherent but the tug of their tempers showing in their tone. Reva's voice wafted upward; she was singing, her voice just high enough to carry clearly above all other sound:

"Oh don't you remember sweet Betsy
    from Pike,
  Who crossed the wide mountains with
    her lover Ike,
With two yoke of oxen, a large yellow dog,
  A tall Shanghai rooster, and one spotted
    hog . . . "

The barkeep left with the tray, and Pearl returned to the window, again making an ungainly silhouette. He stood thoughtfully silent, drumming his fingertips against the pane. Then: "I can't help but wonder . . . " he murmured.

"What now?" Stroud demanded, a sharp edge of irritation to his voice.

"Reva," Pearl said dreamily. "See here, Mace. Peso swears he left Madden looking like dead. But Madden came here this morning. He left word for me with one of the barkeeps — after he'd asked for Peso. Reva didn't ride in until after midnight. I had one of my boys check with the livery stable. Madden got in about half an hour before she did — wearing a bandage under his shirt, according to the hostler."

Stroud moved in the chair, making it creak. "You start wondering about Reva *now?* After the things we've talked in front of her!"

Pearl's voice was still dreamy. "She knows nothing about tonight. I thought that best. I shall keep a closer eye on her from now on." He was looking through the window, his head tilted slightly. "A pair of men riding out together. Settlers, from the cut of them."

Stroud came to the window. "Gunther," he said. "I had a hunch he'd string along." He stood watching, his broad face hardening as a new thought came to him. "Cibo, some of your outfit has been rough on my farmer boys. One lad got dumped into your alley just last night because he called a houseman on a shifty deal at the blackjack table. Stone had to put stitches in his scalp."

Pearl said, "That's one who'll think twice about calling cheat in Cibo Pearl's place."

"Hell," Stroud said, "you can bust up all of them, once we've moved onto Warbonnet. But I may need whole-skinned boys in the meantime."

Pearl bent over his watch for another look. "Twenty minutes," he murmured. "That stage is twenty minutes late!"

"Something's stirring the dust down there," Stroud observed.

"Warbonnet!" Pearl cried and was stricken with terror. His fear showed; he stepped back quickly from the window and seemed to shrink within his collar.

"Hell," Stroud said, disgust in his voice, "it's three-four boys riding in for a night's fun. Hashknife, that's who they are. I recognize that sawed-off horse wrangler of theirs."

Pearl moved again to the window. "Just the same, it's a question whether Warbonnet gets here before the stage arrives." He fumbled a frilly handkerchief from his breast pocket and dabbed at his round, oily face. Sweat stood on him, and his eyes were milky in the half-light.

"What's keeping the girl in town?" Stroud wondered aloud.

"That's what I've wanted to know, Mace. Is it that Ordway's to bring the crew if she doesn't show back at a certain time?"

"I hadn't thought of that," Stroud admitted.

Pearl peered through the window again. "I wish that stage would come."

Stroud cocked his head. "Listen! I thought I heard that old Concord creaking!"

Pearl reached out and gripped Stroud's arm. "It's here!" he cried. "Look below!"

And now down there in the dusty reach between the two rows of falsefronts, an ancient Concord was coming to a stop, the dust of travel silver-gray upon it. The driver set the brake, threw down the reins to a waiting hostler, and descended from his perch. People came drifting out of the night and milled upon the boardwalk before the stage depot, gathering about the stage with a desultory curiosity that had about it a ritual-like reserve. There was sound and movement and an orderly confusion as the six horses were freed from their harness and fresh horses brought at once to replace them. The stage door opened and a man dismounted, showing the stiffness of long travel.

"Only one passenger," Stroud observed without any real interest.

"A stranger," Pearl judged.

A warsack was thrown down from the luggage rack to this lone passenger; he shouldered it and was lost in the shadow of a giant cottonwood growing before the stage depot. The crowd dwindled until there was no crowd.

"What's keeping Barker?" Pearl demanded, his voice fretful again. "He knows the stage stops no longer than it takes to change horses!"

Stroud said, "I told him to keep his distance till the coach was ready to roll. He's off somewhere, watching."

"He'd better come along soon."

"Here he comes now, Cibo."

Two men moved into the dim cone of light cast from the stage depot's window, and one of these was Jess Barker and the other was Rex Willard. They were not handcuffed together, but Barker kept always a pace behind Willard, and about the deputy was an obvious nervousness. They climbed into the coach, Willard first; and when the door had closed behind them, Pearl said elatedly, "No fuss! Not a bit of fuss!" His voice turned shrill again. "Now why don't they get that thing rolling? What is the driver waiting for?"

Stroud turned excited now. "Look, Cibo! Look!"

"The girl!" Pearl ejaculated. "Mace, what in the devil — ?"

Corinna Willard was down there; she was speaking briefly to the driver, who'd started climbing to his perch. She paused, the door of the coach open and her foot lifted to the step; she began talking to someone inside, Barker probably, for she gesticulated angrily. Then she climbed inside and closed the door. The driver cracked his whip, the sound carrying to the room above like a dim ghost of itself. The dust began roiling, and the coach rolled from view.

Pearl again dragged out his handkerchief and mopped at his face. His voice was stunned and unbelieving. "She's going along!"

"Her tough luck," Stroud said.

Cibo Pearl thought about this, and from the run of his thoughts came his first composure of the evening. "Yes," he said and shrugged. "Her tough luck."

"I think," said Stroud and began groping toward the door, "we'd better get downstairs, the two of us, and have a game of poker — a long game. We'll want plenty of people remembering where we were when that murderer gets dragged off the coach and hanged to the nearest tree." He got the door opened.

Pearl asked then, "Where will it happen?"

Stroud shrugged. "I left that to the Peso Kid."

"There is just one thing still bothering me," Pearl said. "Why didn't Warbonnet show? What has happened to Tucker Ordway, Mace?"

Again Stroud shrugged. "Our good luck," he said.

The lone passenger who'd alighted from the stage started along the boardwalk making a lazy sort of search for a hotel and giving little sign that he was alert to all the town, its shadows and its small sounds and the things that made its personality. He was a tall man, as tall almost as Madden, and at least twenty years older, a weathered man with a face that looked naked, for the sun had bleached his brows to a neutral hue. His nose was ample, his eyes gray and grim and thoughtful. He walked a dozen paces, then set down his warsack and stood studying the passers-by, letting three homesteaders clump on before accosting a horse-and-rope man.

"Swap the makings for a light," the stranger said.

The cowboy obliged him with a match. The stranger thumbed back his sombrero and put the match behind his ear, then lifted Durham from his vest pocket and deftly snapped up a quirly. Afterwards, he passed the sack. "Where does Warbonnet lie from here?"

"North, mostly," the cowhand said. "It crowds the west hills."

"Make it by midnight?"

"Not tonight."

"Feller named Willard ramrodding it?"

The cowboy grinned. He was young and a little drunk. "Some say yes."

"Might he be in town?"

"He is. Under lock and key."

"So?" said the stranger and was startled.

"Thanks for the tobacco," the cowboy said, returning the sack. The stranger tucked the Durham away and stopped to lift his warsack, letting his informant drift on. But with the sack hoisted to his shoulder, the stranger still stood in the same spot, his face screwed tight with his thinking. Then he eased the warsack to a more comfortable position and began walking again. But with that slight movement his arm brushed back his vest and the lamplight from the doorways set aglitter a bit of badge thus revealed, the shield-shaped badge of a United States federal marshal.

9. To Stop a Stage

Madden had gone from Luddington's room to his own and stretched himself upon the bed. He lay there with his hands clasped at the back of his neck; he lay staring at the ceiling, his body tired and his thoughts sluggish.

He turned over in his mind what Luddington had said about Rex Willard, and he supposed there was sense to it, and his old resentment against all that was Warbonnet arose. He thought: *Hell, which side am I fighting on?* He was of half a mind to go back along the hall and tell Luddington that he'd changed his plans and there'd be no defending Rex Willard at Yellow Lodge.

But still he lay, and when he closed his eyes, a picture came to him strongly, the picture of Corinna as she'd looked this morning with the dust of travel on her and the fear in her eyes. That was what made the difference.

He dozed then and awoke to find the room gray with twilight. He went to the dining room and had a solitary meal; Luddington was taking supper, too; but they still played at being only chance acquaintances, and he gave Luddington a nod, no more than that. Jess Barker came in and took a corner table and ate hurriedly, then toted a tray with him from the hotel. That would be for Willard, Madden knew. Presently Luddington left, and Madden supposed the lawyer was going to the Palace for his evening's poker. Madden considered going there himself, recalling the Peso Kid and the score still to be settled. But the Kid knew by now that Larry Madden lived, and the Kid, Madden judged, would be lying low.

Again he climbed the stairs to his room, and once inside he left the lamp unlighted. He looked at the bed; he'd got mighty tired of that bed. He drew the one chair to the window and sat there and built up a quirly and watched the street below, having thus a balcony seat to Sawtelle's night life. He saw the pattern of light and shadow that lay upon the boardwalks and the roiled dust between them; he saw riders drift in, the hoofs on their horses lifting the dust and making it a yellow mist.

He thought of getting his own horse and going riding, but there was nowhere in particular to ride. He remembered Reva and all she'd said to him as they'd parted the night before. He recalled Reva's classic profile and the dignity that was hers, and he thought then of Cibo Pearl, fat and oily; and he put the quirly to the floor and ground it hard beneath his boot.

At once he made up another cigarette, and while he smoked and watched the street, the Peso Kid came riding below.

The sight of that slim youngster brought Madden to his feet. He put his hands to the window sash to raise it higher, and his intention was to call to the Kid from here; he would have it out with the Kid. He had the window half raised when he changed his mind. If he made a challenge, the Kid would start gunning, and he would have to fire at the Kid in return, and in such an exchange it was always some bystander who stopped lead. He turned to the door and went down the stairs quickly.

When he came out upon the boardwalk the Kid was gone from sight, swallowed by the dark end of the street. The Kid had been heading eastward, and he'd sat his saddle like a man with business on his mind. Madden gave this his brief speculation, and then, on impulse, he hurried up the boardwalk to the livery and got his own horse. When he rose to saddle, he cut along the side of the livery stable and picked his way behind the buildings, sometimes coming between them almost to the street to look again. The Kid hadn't turned back. This process brought Madden surreptitiously to the east end of the street.

Here, where the street now became a road, a dust wake lifted. Someone had passed out of town not very long ago. The Kid?

Madden walked his horse along the road until the fever of chase began working in him, and he lifted the mount to a trot. This pace sent pain along his left side. He held the horse to a walk then. He hoped that Peso was in no great hurry, and he fell to wondering what had taken the Kid in this direction.

In the old days there had been a stage road angling down off the western hills and cutting in a southeasterly direction into Sawtelle, but that had been in an era when mines were worked high in the hills and the traffic had been heavy and Summit House had been a way station with a roistering life. The old road had long since been abandoned. The new stage road ran straight from west to east, cutting across the lower end of the valley and passing through Sawtelle to skirt the southernmost hills that were the Beavertail's eastern wall. Beyond, a good sixty miles to the east, lay Yellow Lodge. If the Kid were on his way to the county seat, his trip must tie up with Rex Willard and the coming trial, Madden reflected, and he wondered what dark purpose the Kid was supposed to serve.

Shortly two horsemen came clattering along the road behind Madden, holding their horses to a stiff trot. When they drew abreast, he saw from the cut of their clothes and the awkward way they jolted in their saddles that they were settlers. They gave him sidelong glances as they went by, their gaze a little too intent for his liking, but one of them said with gruff courtesy, "Good evening." Madden returned the salutation, and they moved on past. One looked back over his shoulder, then spoke to the other. Madden wondered if these two had been among the bunch who'd harassed Rex Willard that first night and were now recognizing him, Madden, for who he was.

He decided then to draw slightly aside from the road, but he kept moving, paralleling the road and waiting to see if either of the settlers turned back. The country here to the east of Sawtelle was flat; long, grassy meadows stretched on either side of the road, with occasional tree clumps showing as Madden drew nearer to the hills. The moon had not yet risen enough to make more than a dim silver thread of the road. It was a good country for riding and a good night; and excitement had taken hold of Madden, giving him a zest that sloughed off the early evening's boredom.

All of five miles out of Sawtelle, he heard

the muted thunder of more riders to the rear, and shortly three came along at a punishing pace, making a tight group. These were also sod busters; Madden, wondering, watched them go by. The land was roughening now and beginning to tilt upward, and the timber was becoming thicker. A breeze flowed downhill, stirring Madden's neckerchief and lifting the mane of his horse. He rode on; the timber began crowding close to the road and made of it a black gully through the forest, and Madden had to pick his way carefully through the thickness of pine. Another rider came along, this one alone; he passed within a dozen feet of Madden, not seeing him.

For a few minutes Madden sat his saddle then, listening to the silence of the night that was somehow not quite a silence, having in it the tiny alien shards of sound, the lingering lost echoes of men traveling; and he put his speculation on all this and found it baffling. The Peso Kid represented Cibo Pearl, and the settlers had proved themselves pawns of Mace Stroud. Since Pearl and Stroud had common cause, there might be some kinship of interest among all these travelers who headed along the Yellow Lodge road this night.

Madden wondered what that kinship could be and found no answer that fitted. But his curiosity was constant now, and from it came a new purpose. His plan had been to overtake the Kid somewhere out here in the night and settle for what had happened on Circle M yesterday. Now he was more concerned with knowing what business brought so many men into the hills.

His next thought was to continue following the road, staying behind the last traveler but keeping close enough so that he might be on hand to see whatever transpired. There was a danger in this; there might be still other settlers coming up behind. He could keep to the timber, but now he was deep in first-growth pine, a nearly impenetrable palisade. Then he took to thinking about the road; he'd once trailed some of his own cattle over it to the railroad at Yellow Lodge, and he recalled that the road climbed these hills in a series of gigantic switchbacks, thus keeping always at a gentle pitch.

Remembering this, he turned away from the road to feel his way back into the timber. Soon there was less underbrush, and sometimes there was wide openness, and then he was through the timber to the steeper slope of the hillside, and he began climbing this.

Once again he was gambling; there was no assurance that he could scale the slope to where the road, after hairpinning, reached a new level. His horse showed reluctance for the ascent, and Madden had frequently to use his spurs. Before long, the horse was heaving beneath him, but by then they were fifty feet upgrade. Madden dismounted and clambered on upward, jerking at the reins to keep the horse following him, speaking softly and urgently to the horse. Sometimes Madden found handholds on bushes, and always he had to dig his boot toes into the rocky loam of the slope, and his hurt side began aching again.

Halfway up he wondered at the wisdom of this notion. He became convinced that though he could make it himself, he might have to abandon the horse. He had his choice between climbing on alone or turning back to the lower road, and neither choice was to his liking. He might need the horse above. He began moving laterally along the face of the slope, looking for a gentler pitch; and at last he found one and rose up over the hump, still leading the horse.

Now he was on the upper road, and he stood panting for breath while the horse blew itself. Then Madden looked and saw the dust wake on the road and decided that one rider had passed. The Peso Kid — ? That seemed likely, for the Kid had been the first out of Sawtelle of the group that interested Madden.

He looked down from the road; he could

see a black mass of pine tops and, far to the west, out there in the yonder openness, the twinkling lights of the town. Cold wind sifted down from the hill's crest, and the stars stood out. He looked along the road in both directions and nothing disturbed the night. He made an estimate of time and distance and called on his memory of the switchbacks and guessed that he was perhaps half an hour ahead of the six who'd trailed the Peso Kid out of Sawtelle.

He frowned, still puzzled as to what had brought those seven into the night, and as he frowned, he heard a faint sound from below, a distant, almost-lost clatter. A wagon, he guessed, and instantly began wondering about it. Then the sound reached him again and he revised his guess, remembering that a stagecoach ran this road to Yellow Lodge. He supposed they'd be putting Rex Willard on that coach one of these nights.

He remembered the sod busters, so awkward in their saddles, finding it hard work to ride, and he thought: *Now why didn't the fools wait and take the coach?*

He listened hard for the hoofbeats of those six and heard nothing. He had put himself between them and the Kid by this climb, and he began riding slowly along, following the Kid's tracks on upward but stopping often to listen for the six behind him. After a half hour there was still silence. Peso's dust was settling, which meant the Kid was covering distance faster than Madden.

Madden reined up and again keened the night; and then, with his decision made more of instinct than of reason, he turned and began riding back downhill. He reached the place where he had ascended to this higher road and went on half a mile below it, following the curves of the road as it looped along this shelf on the hillside. And so he came upon the six.

They were together now, a tight huddle of horsemen sitting their saddles on the inner side of the road, the high slope above them making a shadow in which they were nearly lost. One of them was smoking, his cigarette a faint pin-point in the night, and this was what gave Madden his knowledge of their presence. Drawing to the inner side of the road, he dismounted and left his horse with reins trailing and moved forward on foot, certain that they must have heard his coming. Then he heard the stagecoach and understood; it was toiling along down the road, not far below the group, and the attention of all of them was turned in that direction. He made his guess as to how close the coach now was, and hugging close to the slope, he got to within speaking distance of the six.

One of them said, "Here she comes," and his voice was strained with excitement. "Gunther, you'd better speak up. Can we count on you?"

Another, Gunther, said, "I don't know, Sam. This ain't our kind of doings. He was my kin, and I keep remembering that, but I keep remembering, too, that we got no call to be mixed up in this."

The first speaker said, "She's almost here. Either we let her go by, or we don't."

This Gunther made an ungainly shape in a saddle. He made a sort of hunching movement with his shoulders, and then he said, "I've come this far. I might as well go through with it, Sam."

"Shucks," Sam said. "Now you're talking sense!"

And then the stagecoach's dust was a blur of silver in the starshine, and the coach loomed up, the horses straining against the slant; and Madden heard the explosive pop of the driver's whip. He took a step forward and got his gun into his hand and said in a carrying voice, "Easy, boys!"

That made all six of them swing their heads his way, and the surprise of one was so great that he was moved to astonished ejaculation. "That feller was behind us down below!" he blurted. "Now how in the name of Nick — ?"

Madden came closer and said, "Just sit your saddles, boys, and keep your hands on the horns. That's right! Play it peaceful, and you'll all live to tell your wives about it. You, over there to the left! Get your hands where I can see them!"

The coach went toiling by, and to the high-perched driver this must have looked like a group of horsemen waiting by the roadside to give him room to pass, for he lifted his hand in salute. Madden raised his free hand in turn and got an indistinct glimpse of a passenger's face as the coach wheeled on. The dust rose chokingly, and Madden tasted it upon his lips.

He waited until the coach's clatter was dim with distance, then said, "Down from those horses! All of you!"

They dismounted silently, and stood grouped together; he made a motion with his gun for them to spread out, and they did so. He could see the hard shine of their eyes, and he read their anger and fear, but none of them were foolhardy. He brought two fingers to his lips and whistled, and this fetched his horse to him. Into the saddle, he moved carefully forward and gathered up the reins of the six waiting horses, tucking the loose lines under his left arm and still keeping his gun-hand free.

122

He did this with the silent attention of the men upon him, and he sat his saddle then and looked down at them. They were weathered men, all, unused to the ways of violence and filled now with grave uncertainties.

Madden said, "You're going to walk, boys. All the way back to town. Unless you want to tell me beforehand what fetched you."

All of them stirred, but none spoke; and Madden, remembering the name of one, said, "Gunther — ?"

Gunther looked up; he was a great, shaggy man with a look of stubborn tenacity and slow temper to him.

"What was it, Gunther?" Madden demanded, his voice suddenly a whiplash. "A holdup? I don't think so. That coach hasn't carried anything worth stealing since the mines closed years ago."

Gunther spread a huge pair of hands and said, "We figure it ain't right there should be one kind of justice for poor men and another kind for rich ones."

The gun spoke then, far up the road where the stage had vanished, the report making only a small flutter of sound. Madden suddenly remembered the Kid; and remembering, he tied the Kid to what Gunther had just said, and he understood everything then and called himself a fool for not having under-

123

stood before. The Kid riding out and a half dozen coming after him, coming in twos and threes to await the Yellow Lodge coach. Coming to do a chore for which at least one had had small stomach. They had intended to stop the stage because Rex Willard was on it — Willard, who might stand a chance at a Yellow Lodge trial but would stand no chance in the night and the hills. It was as simple as that.

And now the Kid's gun spoke again, up there above, and that was when Madden remembered Corinna's saying that when Rex Willard went to Yellow Lodge, she would be going, too.

10. Warbonnet

The horses gave Madden the devil's own choice — the six captured horses of the sod busters — for Madden's need was to get on up the road after that stagecoach, but if he abandoned the horses for the sake of speed, he gave Gunther and the others the means of buying back into this. Therefore he made a quick compromise, dumping his gun into its holster and transferring the spare reins to his right hand. Wheeling his own horse, he started up the road at a high gallop, trailing the other horses after him. At once he was in trouble. Some of the horses caught the contagion of his urgency and bolted ahead; some dragged stubbornly on the reins. Madden was in a pocket of dust and noise and confusion, pitting all of a cowboy's skill at trying to keep himself from becoming hopelessly entangled.

Around the first turn, he let a couple of the horses go, sorting out a pair that had showed reluctance. Then he galloped on, releasing two more farther up the road. When he came to where he'd made the ascent up the slope, he let the last two go. Freed, some of the horses kept running, while others fell to cropping the sparse grass by the road's edge.

Madden's hope now was that if the six men he'd left behind elected to have a hand in this, it would take them some time to recover all the horses and get mounted. In the meantime, unencumbered, he was spurring on up the road; the slope to his left and the drop to his right became blurs, but this hard riding hadn't brought him as far as he'd scouted the upper road earlier, when he came around a curve and found the stopped stagecoach before him. The Peso Kid was here, too, and this meant that the Kid, like himself, had turned back down the road.

The driver made a black blotch upon his high perch, and lined beside the stagecoach were three people. Madden judged them to be Willard and Corinna and could only guess at the other one, until he realized it must be Jess Barker. Still another man sat a saddle, holding a gun on the passengers, and that one was the Peso Kid. The Kid was doing no more than this, and in the Kid's passivity Madden saw the pattern of Peso's play.

Those shots had been to stop the stage and intimidate driver and passengers; now the Kid was waiting for the men who were to have joined him for the finish. That was why the

Kid had turned back down the road, narrowing the distance between himself and Gunther's bunch. And the Kid, hearing the clatter of many hoofs on the road, must have presumed that the six were coming up. Thus the Kid was set for a surprise, but he'd kept half his wariness, for he was peering hard as Madden rode up. The Kid made a quick, jerking motion, a man enlivened to his danger, and snapped a frantic shot at Madden.

Madden's own gun had been in his hand since he'd freed himself of the spare reins. Feeling the airlash of the Kid's bullet, he swerved in his saddle and sent a shot of his own. This high country caught the beat of the guns and hammered out echoes, flinging them far and near. At once the stage horses were rearing and pitching, and the driver risked lowering his hands to fight their fractiousness. Two of the dark forms beside the stagecoach blended into one in a mighty tussling, and Madden guessed that Willard had jumped Jess Barker and was after the deputy's gun. But Madden's real concern was to get the Kid, and he fired again.

The Kid's horse made a flinching, sideward jump; the Kid sawed at the reins and swung the horse about and went careening on up the road. Madden fired once more, but as he spurred his own horse forward and came abreast of the stagecoach, the Kid was rounding a curve above and was lost then to sight.

Willard said, from the banked shadows, "Madden, eh? You needn't worry. I've drawn the teeth of this one," and Madden now saw that Jess Barker lay in a crumpled heap on the road. Corinna stood stiffly, her face a white smudge in the shadows. She seemed to sway on her feet; she leaned back against the coach, bracing her shoulders.

Madden was at once out of his saddle, and he punched fresh cartridges into his gun as he walked quickly to the rim of the road and looked down. The slope here was gentler than where he had ascended; he could see the moon-burnished gray of shale and below that the dark jungle of pine tops. He gave the slope his quick and careful attention, finished with his gun and dropped it into leather, then came back around the coach and grasped Corinna's elbow.

"Up into my saddle," he said.

She obeyed him, and when she'd mounted, he turned to Willard and said, "You and I will have to go afoot. Down the slope. It's not as bad as it looks."

Willard shook his head. "See her back to Warbonnet, Madden, and thanks. I couldn't talk her out of coming. I'm going on to Yellow Lodge."

Madden said with no patience, "Don't be a fool!"

"Don't you understand?" Willard said. "If I run, I make myself a fugitive."

"If you stay, you make yourself a dead man," Madden snapped. "The Kid will be back here as soon as he catches his breath. And there are six men coming up the road. They mean to put a rope around your neck. I haven't time to argue with you. Are you coming, or do I have to lay my gun-barrel between your horns and tie you behind my saddle?"

Corinna looked down at them. "Please, Rex, do as he says!"

Willard stood hesitant for a moment, a man weighing idealism against logic, then moved around the stagecoach toward the slope. Barker was struggling to his feet. Madden got the deputy by the collar and helped him to a stand, then pinned him hard against the coach.

"Look," Madden said, his voice brittle, "they couldn't have planned this thing without counting on you. For that, I'm going to have your badge torn off. But meantime you can go back to Stroud or Pearl or whoever planned this necktie party and tell them it didn't work. Then clear out of the country mighty fast!"

He slapped Barker then, a backhanded

blow that caught the deputy alongside the head and took the legs out from under him, spilling him to the road again. Madden looked up at the driver. "You can haul this part of your load on to Yellow Lodge or leave it lying, as you wish."

The driver was an old man, turned neutral in all things by the creeping years. He spat. "I just tool the coach. The passengers make up their own minds."

Madden nodded. He stood keening the night for hoofbeats, and the breeze bore to him some ghosts of sounds from far down the road, dim and untranslatable. He took the saddler's reins in his hands and said to Willard, "Come on," and they edged over the rim and began the descent. That first hump was a hard one; Corinna clutched the saddlehorn, her chin snapping against her chest.

Once they were beyond the shale, she said, "Let me have the reins. I think I can do better if I handle the horse myself."

Madden handed the leather up to her, saying nothing.

Then they were slipping and sliding downward; at some places Corinna had to dismount and lead the horse. Madden found the descent harder than the climbing had been, but he had come down off Tumbling Wall once; and this was easy traveling compared to Tumbling

Wall, which had taxed his strength and his ingenuity and given him many moments of wild fear. Soon they got into timber and threshed through underbrush until they found a game trail. Now the sky was lost to them, blanketed out by the interlaced boughs above, but they followed the trail downward and in due course came to the lower road.

Madden's side was aching again, and he was beginning to feel the weight of the hours and the miles and the constant pitch of excitement. On the road he paused again, listening. He said then, "They're not on the slope. If they come back around the switchback, we've got an edge of time. Willard, climb up behind Corinna. I'll hang back here and see if I can keep them busy."

Corinna said, "We're not budging unless you come along, Larry."

Madden frowned. "That means we go no faster than a walking man."

Corinna said, "Do you think you own all the pride in the world?"

He thought about this and had to grin. "Let's get moving," he said and started trudging down the road.

Willard walked beside him, and Corinna paced them on the horse. Willard turned once and asked that she go on ahead; she made him some low-voiced answer that escaped Madden, and after that Willard did no more entreating. They threaded along that dark gully of a road, with the pines hemming them on either side, and frequently Madden called a halt while he listened intently, sometimes getting down to press his ear to the road. At last he said, "Here they come now." He grasped the bridle and hauled the horse off the road into the trees, where the three huddled together and waited until a group of riders walked their horses past.

"Six," Madden counted softly. "Six men — but two of them are doubled on one horse. That makes one they didn't catch."

Willard said, "Those were the men you spoke of?"

"All but the Peso Kid. If any one of them tried the slope, it would be the Kid. I'd say from the looks of that bunch that they've had enough. But the Kid will keep hunting till you reach Warbonnet's gate."

They attained the road again and moved along it, Madden still pausing frequently, no longer concerned about Gunther's bunch, who were now ahead and covering distance faster than the three, but wondering about the Kid, wondering where the Kid kept himself. The Kid had that Indian look of one who could smell out a trail.

Deep darkness came and then the first light

132

outlined the hills; shadows turned pale, and when grayness seeped over the land, they were out of timber, and Sawtelle was within their sight far down the road. Here Madden quitted the road again, leading his party due north.

"You're not going into town?" Willard asked.

Madden shook his head. "Do you like the inside of that calaboose? We'll borrow horses at Hashknife."

Willard seemed about to make protest, but whatever was in his mind he left unvoiced. Willard looked dog-tired; he lurched as he walked.

Madden said, "You might as well ride behind that saddle for a while."

"I'll walk," Willard said.

They came into Hashknife's yard in midmorning, the two men walking, and at this southernmost of the ranches abutting the Beavertail's eastern wall, they borrowed three saddlers, Madden exchanging his own tired horse for a fresh mount after making arrangements to swap back at the Sawtelle livery. They had breakfast at Hashknife, no man asking them a question with other than his eyes; and then they lined out across the valley for Warbonnet. The land lay bright, and dew sparkled in the grass. They skirted the settlers' wire, riding north of it, and saw no rider who might have challenged them, and they came at long last to Warbonnet's gate where rifle barrels glinted in the sun as two of the crew stood guard.

Here Madden drew rein. "I'll leave you now."

Willard said, "Man, there's blood showing through your shirt! You're coming to the ranch and rest and have yourself taken care of before you ride on."

Madden's jaw tightened. "I'll come through Warbonnet's wire one of these days. This isn't the day."

Willard said, "Who's the fool now?"

Only then, with his chore completed, did Madden realize how much the night had taken out of him, and he knew that he wanted nothing better than to ease himself into a bunk and get his boots off; but the old pride and the old stubbornness were strong in him, ruling him, until Corinna said, "Larry, please . . . It doesn't mean that you'll see Dad. Not unless you want to."

He looked at her; he saw her concern in her eyes, and it softened him just a little. He said, "Only to the bunkhouse. I'm not stopping under Warbonnet's roof."

Corinna said, "As you wish it."

And so Madden entered Warbonnet's gate

and walked a horse along Warbonnet's road to the great gaunt house that Tucker Ordway had built, and he stumbled into Warbonnet's empty bunkhouse and rolled into a bunk, too tired to care about his boots or to expend the energy to remove them. Sleep came at once, wafting him to the sweetest oblivion he had ever known, and he had time only for one last conscious thought. He was remembering Corinna and Willard and how it had come about that he, Madden, was here, and he thought: *Damned if the cards weren't stacked!*

He awoke to find the gray of twilight at the windows, and the yard astir with sound and movement, and a gray-bearded man bending over him. The man said gruffly, "I'll have a look at your side," and Madden recognized him as Doc Stone. He supposed that the Willards had had the doctor fetched out during the day, and he was annoyed, not liking being obligated to Warbonnet, but he let the medico cleanse the wound again and rebandage it.

Stone said, "You'd better keep to a bed, or you'll be busting yourself open faster than I can tie you up." He took his black bag and left.

Madden came to a stand and discovered that he was feeling fine. His boots had been removed as he slept; he found them and stomped into them. He came out into the yard and saw the crew lounging about, in from their day's riding; he gave them sidelong glances, mindful that Luddington had said that strange men had asked the way to War-bonnet. This crew was a salty one, but it didn't look hardcase. Madden walked at once to the corral and helped himself to a rope and laid it on the horse he'd borrowed from Hash-knife. He got gear onto the mount and was leading it toward the patio when Willard came toward him. Willard looked as though he'd slept some since Madden had last seen him.

Willard said, "You're going?"

Madden nodded.

"But you'll have supper first."

Madden said, "Look, do you think I'd have come through that gate if I hadn't been dead beat out?"

Willard considered this, then said, "What you did last night, you did for her sake; I know that. And I strung along for her sake, too. But whatever good I did by riding into Sawtelle with Jess Barker, I undid. Now I'm an escaped prisoner, and that gives Stroud his excuse to turn his settlers loose against War-bonnet. Still, that doesn't change the fact that you saved my life again. I've hoped that we might be friends. You don't want it that way, I think."

Madden said, "You're Warbonnet."

Willard stepped back a pace, his own kind of pride in his face. "We keep the gate guarded all hours. Hap Sutton's out front. He'll ride down with you and see that they let you through."

"Thanks," Madden said.

He moved past Willard and led his horse around to the front of the ranchhouse, and not finding Sutton here, he waited. Sutton came out of the house. Madden had known him from the old days; he was as much a part of Warbonnet as Tucker Ordway or the native stock that ranged under Ordway's brand. He was a little man, saddle-warped, with a prairie squint to his eyes and a hipshot way of standing. He looked at Madden and said, "Tuck wants a few words with you."

Madden said, "All I'm looking for is the gate. A man gets too many words on this spread."

Sutton said, "I just deliver the messages. You can take it or leave it lay. My guess is that you'll leave it lay. You'll figure that you won't stand so tall in front of a man like Tuck Ordway."

Madden saw the ruse in this, and it was so obvious that he had to grin. "Come to think of it," he said, "I want a few words with Tuck Ordway myself. In fact, I've been wanting

137

them a long, long time. Let's go see how tall *he* stands."

"Come along," Sutton said and turned and mounted the gallery steps.

Madden let the reins drop and followed him, bobbing through the doorway of Warbonnet's ranchhouse. He stood then beneath the roof that Tucker Ordway had wrought; he stood waiting, and he judged then that he hadn't slept enough after all. His hands had a tremble to them, and in the hush of the house he heard the beating of his own heart.

11. Man in the Dust

Sutton led him into a large room with hewn rafters and a stone fireplace so massive that Madden might have stood erect in its black, empty maw. Madden raised his hand, thinking to remove his sombrero, then lowered it lest the common courtesy seem to hold deference. All the room's shades were drawn, though the lamps were not yet lighted, and thus gloom made the interior indistinguishable. This at once turned Madden keenly wary; he stopped in the room's center and stood there until he could make out the woven rugs upon the floor, a huge, round table and a scattering of rawhide-bottomed chairs. The inside walls hadn't been finished off; the chinking between the logs glimmered whitely. Over the fireplace hung the oil portrait of Tucker Ordway.

Madden lifted his eyes to the painting, finding it hard to see and wishing that Sutton would light a lamp. Tucker Ordway's face looked at him from the canvas, broad and blocky, fierce and compelling, the hair a

139

leonine mane, the eyebrows bushy, the mouth a grim slash. The artist had caught all of Ordway's driving power, his primitive restlessness; it was the picture of both a man and an era. Peering at it, Madden remembered Cibo Pearl and thought: *Ten thousand hard round dollars!*

Beneath the painting, in a homemade chair set to one side of the fireplace and facing toward the door, Tucker Ordway waited.

His arms rested on the arms of the chair, his broad hands lay open and curled downward, his body had the shapelessness of a heavy man relaxed. His head was lifted to Madden; his gaze was fixed on Madden but gave Madden no special attention, as though Ordway were looking through him rather than at him. He was the man in the painting, yet there was a difference; and Madden sought at once to define the difference, wishing again for lamplight. The picture was of a tree that stood sturdy against the storms; the man was that same tree bowed by the winds and stripped by winter. A solid man of solid convictions had withstood everything but the years.

Seeing him thus, Madden felt cheated; he had come to pit himself against an enemy and found that enemy less formidable than he had been.

Hap Sutton, at Madden's elbow, said, "I fetched him for you, Tuck."

Ordway lifted his right hand. "I won't waste time on you, Madden. I want the answer to one question: What fetched you back to the Beavertail?"

And there the question lay, and with it a challenge, for that had been in Ordway's voice. The answer had been simple and clear in Madden's mind on all the trails up out of Arizona; it had burned in him the evening he'd found his way down off Tumbling Wall. Since then, there'd been many people to confuse his thinking and shake his certainty — Stroud and Pearl and Reva and Corinna, and even Doc Stone. Sometimes he'd forgotten his hatred in the full, dangerous hours; now the edge of it was blunted by seeing this man, seeing what the years had done to him.

But the whip was still here; the huge blacksnake lay coiled on the floor, within reach of Ordway's hand if he bent to seize it. The whip hadn't changed with time; it had lost none of its resiliency, none of its sting. The whip was still here, and so were the marks on Madden's back.

Ordway said again, out of the silence, "What fetched you? Speak up!"

"I came back," Madden said slowly, "to kill you."

Ordway held silent, not stirring; he might have been asleep. The darkness was gathering more deeply in the room, and Madden again wondered about the lamp, and he thought: *Is he sick? Are they afraid I'll see how sick he is?*

But Ordway's voice, breaking the stillness, held all its old strength. "Yes," he said. "Of course. I've known for five years that you'd come back some day. We might as well get it over with. Have you a time and place in mind?"

This came so suddenly that Madden had the feeling of one who had groped forever in the dark only to find the object he sought clutched in his own hand. And he felt, too, that here was a strange thing: he had expected no woman to understand his need to face Ordway with a gun, and he'd spoken of that need to no man save Ames Luddington, lest he seem vindictive. But the one who understood a man's pride was Tucker Ordway himself, and there was nothing left now but for Madden to speak.

Still, there was one thing that stayed him, and he voiced it. "In your day, you were faster with a gun than I ever wanted to be, Ordway. That was then. I'm not sure it would be a fair fight now."

Ordway leaned forward in his chair, his fury in his face. "I can give you cards and spades any day of the week! Are you trying to crawl out of it? Name your time and place!"

"Not at Warbonnet," Madden said. "I don't want your crew on my back the minute you go down. And not in town, where a stray bullet might tag the wrong man. Anywhere else will do."

"They'd try to stop us on the ranch, Corry and her man," Ordway said. He put his fingers to his forehead and sat thinking for a moment. "Will you be at Summit House about sundown tomorrow?"

"I'll be there," Madden said.

Ordway lifted his hand. "Take him out of here, Hap."

Sutton touched Madden's elbow. "That's all, boy."

Madden turned and followed the foreman out of the house and climbed upon his waiting horse. Sutton got a mount and led the way along the road toward the gate. They rode without talk, and in Madden was the trance-like sensation that all that had happened in the house had been a dream, brief and bitter. But when they reached the gate and Warbonnet's gun-guards opened it for Madden, Sutton asked, "You going to be there?"

"You bet," Madden said.

Sutton reached for his makings and busied himself at a cigarette; he spilled some of the tobacco. "Will you take it from an older man that nobody's gonna win?"

Madden said, "All I've got since I came back is too much advice. Look, mister, as it is, I'm settling with Ordway for just half of what I came after." He turned his horse and lifted it to a gallop.

He came down to the valley's floor in the flowing dusk and kept the horse at a high lope until some of his own tempestuousness ran out of him. He thought: *Tomorrow, and it's all done*, and tried to find peace in that thought. He gave his consideration to Tucker Ordway's gun skill; it had been as great as any in the Beavertail in the old days. He gave no thought to losing against that skill; he had waited too long.

Presently he pulled his horse to a walk and rode along, the hills on either hand losing their detail until finally they stood as black silhouettes against the horizons. He rode in the middle valley's vast emptiness, liking the aloneness, liking the night.

He had put Warbonnet five miles behind when he saw a horseman approaching him on the trail, and he was instantly wary, remembering that the Peso Kid might still be questing. But this horseman loomed too big to be the Kid; and when they had drawn close, Madden saw that this one was a stranger, a

144

tall, weathered man, ample of nose. He had a warsack tied behind his saddle, but the horse belonged to Sawtelle's livery stable, for Madden had seen it there.

The stranger reined short as they drew abreast and spoke a cordial, "Howdy." Then: "Swap the makings for a light."

Madden gave him a match, and the stranger lifted out his Durham. "Far to Warbonnet?"

"Follow this trail till it forks; then start climbing," Madden said and threw his hand to the right. "You'll come upon the wire soon."

"Feathergill's the name," said the stranger. "Sam Feathergill."

Madden held silent, not taking the hint to name himself.

Feathergill got a quirly shaped up and fired. "You ride from Warbonnet," he observed, "but your horse packs a different brand."

Madden said, "Does that concern you?"

Feathergill extended the makings, but Madden shook his head. "I'm obliged," Feathergill said and gave Madden a quick sizing-up and rode on past.

Madden watched him go, then jogged his own horse. He was remembering again that strange men were supposed to have come to Warbonnet of late, and he wondered about this one. But he dismissed Sam Feathergill from his mind, not really caring, and rode on.

He reached Sawtelle late in the night and put the Hashknife horse in the livery and found that his own had been returned that evening. One restaurant was still open; he took supper, then went to the Ogallala and at once fell asleep.

He rose late and found Luddington gone from his room. He went down to the dining room, thinking how he had all this long day to last out, thinking of sunset and Summit House and wondering why his anticipation wasn't sharper. He felt edgy; he felt like a man honed for a fight but not sure whom he should fight. He got no taste out of his food and was about to leave when he caught a scrap of conversation from a nearby table.

"Hell," someone said, "I wouldn't kick if it was a white man."

Madden looked from a corner of his eye and saw two townsmen, the only other diners at this mid-morning hour. The second one said, "It's something to remember at election time. The sheriff's just lazy-careless, Clem. As long as *somebody* gets appointed deputy out here, he's satisfied. And it's easier for him if Mace Stroud does the pickin' and saves him the ride."

"But a Mexican!" the other said. "And a

146

hanger-on at Pearl's place at that!"

Madden pushed back his chair and came out to the street and had a quick look along it, his eyes searching for one man. There were the usual bonneted shoppers, and some heavy-shoed settlers from the tent city, and a Rafter-S cowhand coming out of the mercantile with an opened can of tomatoes in his hand. Madden made a quick scan of all these people, not realizing the fullness of his anger till he found his hands trembling. Then he went directly to Stroud's office, a tiny cubicle set down between the mercantile and Syd Baxter's blacksmith shop, and he found Stroud here, behind his desk. The man and the desk were too big for the room, and there was a filing case, a squat iron safe and a stove besides.

Stroud looked up, his eyes at first alarmed, and then they squinted down, hiding everything, and Stroud's grin broke wide. "Well, Larry — ?"

"I hear it told," Madden said, "that the Peso Kid's just been appointed deputy."

Stroud still took refuge in his pretended affability but his florid face was both wary and hard. "Barker was no man for the job, Larry. You know that. The Kid can be rough if there's a call to be rough."

"That's so," Madden said with a great calmness. "Where is he now?"

"Gone out on a little official business."

Madden leaned forward, putting both palms down on the desk and bringing his face close to Stroud's. "Did he have time to tell you what happened on the Yellow Lodge road night before last?"

The grin left Stroud, and the affability, and he took on a blustery mien. "I'm fighting Warbonnet, Larry. That should be your fight, too. Why are you always showing up at the wrong place at the wrong time? Which side you on, anyway?"

Madden said, "Tell me just one thing, Mace: Did you know that Corinna went out on that stage, too?"

A corner of Stroud's mouth jerked. "Nobody invited her to the party. That was her tough luck."

Madden hit him then. He drove his right fist hard into Stroud's face, spilling him over backward. At once Madden was clambering over the desk, and he leaped full upon Stroud. Stroud got his big arms around him, and the two writhed upon the floor, rolling over and over. Only then did Madden remember his injured side; he had forgotten it in the red haze of anger. Stroud was playing havoc with his ribs, and Madden knew that he must break free of the man.

He worked one hand up to Stroud's face, putting the heel of that hand against Stroud's jaw and pushing at Stroud's nose with his fingers. Stroud shrieked and let go his hold. Instantly Madden rolled away from him. Stroud got on hands and knees and came at him, breathing hard; but Madden put his boot against Stroud's chest and shoved, bringing Stroud against the office safe. The breath whooshed out of Stroud, but he was on his feet almost as quickly as Madden.

They stood then swinging at each other.

Here the advantage was Madden's; he could move faster than Stroud, and his arms were longer. He maneuvered Stroud wherever he wanted him, punishing the man and taking punishment, for Stroud's blows were meaty and some of them got through. He backed Stroud to the desk and bowled him over it with a hard, clean uppercut. Stroud landed heavily, and Madden thought that was the end of it; but Stroud pulled himself to his feet, his mouth bloody, and careened blindly into the stove. The pipes came down with a clatter, and soot was everywhere, and Stroud stood weaving on his feet, dazedly contemplating the stove. He turned and stared at Madden.

Madden asked, "Had enough?"

Some sense came into Stroud's eyes, and a

wild sort of desperation. He clawed for the gun he wore, but his holster had got twisted awry in the struggle and the gun stuck for a moment. Madden came over the desk as Stroud fought the gun clear. Madden bore Stroud backward to the wall, feeling for the man's right wrist and twisting hard. The gun fell to the floor, and Stroud went to his knees after it. Madden got his heel on Stroud's wrist and put all his weight down. Stroud cried out and rolled away from Madden, who instantly kicked the gun to a far corner. Stroud came to his hands and knees and scuttled toward the door. He made it; he got out upon the boardwalk, still moving like a gigantic crab.

Madden cried, "Wait a minute!" and lurched after him.

Stroud got up then, his broken face showing his consciousness that now the fight had been carried to where all the town could see. His face grew more desperate with his humiliation; his anger sharpened. He brought up his fists as Madden came at him again; he fetched Madden a hard blow alongside the head.

Madden shook his head and bore at Stroud, forcing him backward off the boardwalk out into the dust of the street. Madden followed after him, driving Stroud steadily backward, hitting at Stroud again and again with only a dim consciousness that every passer-by had stopped to look, men gathering in tight knots and holding silent. This was not the kind of fight that brought cheers and advice; here were two men trying hard to kill each other.

Madden battered Stroud down to his knees, and Stroud fell over, then got to his hands and knees again and tried once more to scuttle away, stirring the dust and floundering along. Madden caught up with him and jerked at his collar and got Stroud to a stand.

Stroud said, "Damn you!" and it was a blubbery sound.

Stroud lifted his fists again, but Madden smashed through that clumsy guard and got another clean one at Stroud's jaw. Stroud seemed to dissolve before him, going down to lie shapeless in the dust. Madden stood over him, sucking hard for wind, shaking his head to get the buzzing out of it. He toed Stroud with his boot; Stroud did not stir.

For a moment Madden stood reeling on his feet, finding it hard to fix his eyes on anything. He scrubbed his lips with the back of his hand; he looked at his knuckles and found them bloody. His wounded side was soggy with blood again, and breathing was labor.

He supposed he'd better see Doc Stone about his side, and he turned and stumbled away, heading for the medico's home. He was afraid his knees would buckle, and he put all his resolution into walking. That was what he wanted Sawtelle to remember, that one man had lain sprawled in the dust and one man had walked away.

12. The Devil's Deputy

Of the Peso Kid it might have been argued that he possessed a high courage or none at all, for courage implies imagination enough for its possessor to realize his peril and to face it. On this morning the Kid rode the dawn-fresh openness of the Beavertail as imperturbably as he would have taken any other trail, yet his destination was Warbonnet; and this same Kid, the night before last, had ordered Rex Willard from a stagccoach at gunpoint. The man who rode with the Kid was mindful of this; and though he was a dogged man who would have carried his convictions to the gates of doom, he showed uneasiness. He was Gunther, and he was here by his own choice.

Not so the Kid. The Kid had got his orders from Stroud and Pearl. Gunther had been in on that session, and so had several other settlers from the tent city outside Sawtelle. Stroud had found a badge and pinned it onto

153

Peso; Jess Barker had taken his own badge with him when he'd gone on to Yellow Lodge by coach, thus signifying that he'd found the lawing of Sawtelle too big a bite to chew. They had made the Kid the new law, not wasting much time at ritual, and sent him to speak a piece to Warbonnet — and Gunther had asked to go along. Gunther, the kinsman of a man felled in the Beavertail and buried on the flats to the south of Sawtelle.

The Kid rode with his dark young face showing nothing; and if he smarted, no man could have told it. There had been an earlier session with Stroud and Pearl, and Gunther hadn't been present at that one. There had been a report made of a plan foiled, the admission that Rex Willard still lived and, moreover, was now free. Stroud had fumed and laid some nasty names to the Kid; but Pearl, a wiser man, had seen how to shape opportunity out of failure.

Moreover, Pearl had spoken to the Kid on another matter, making mention of ten thousand dollars. If the Kid reflected this morning on such a sum and what it would purchase in the way of dark pleasures, his face showed nothing of this, either.

And so they rode, this odd pair, the man born to the plow and peace, the youth who dealt death, the one solid and clumsy in a saddle, the other lithe and graceful and part of his horse — Gunther troubled with the temerity of this mission and troubled, too, by his choice of allies; the Kid showing no more concern than a horse shows when a guiding hand sets its course.

They faced toward Tumbling Wall through the long morning and came to Warbonnet's wire by high noon and followed the fence to a gate where two men sat their saddles with rifles ready. Of these two the Kid inquired politely: "*Senor* Willard? He ees home, no?"

"He's home," one of the guards admitted, giving the Kid a sharp appraisal and looking southward then. "What do you want with him?"

"I am the law, *amigo*," said the Kid and lifted his vest to touch his new badge with a thumb.

The guard looked shocked by this, but his contempt grew no less. He spat, then turned to his companion. "Now I've seen everything!"

Gunther spoke up, his voice a deep rumble. "All we want with your boss is words. He ain't afraid of them, is he?"

The first guard thought this over, his eyes wary and his face troubled. He said, "You take them on up to the house, Steve." He looked at Gunther and the Kid. "Shuck your guns first."

"I carry no weapon," said Gunther.

The Peso Kid shrugged, lifting his six-shooter from its holster and letting it fall to the ground. His horse shied from the glitter, and he quieted the horse with a quick, vicious jerking at the bit. He had a knife scabbard in his right boot, and the hilt of a bowie showed. He pointed to the knife and said, "You want thees also?" and laughed at them with his eyes.

"Never mind," said the guard.

The gate was opened; and the one remained beside it while the other, Steve, led the way up the winding road to the timber and through it to the ranchhouse. They came to a halt before the long low building, and Steve stepped down from his saddle. The Kid did likewise, following Steve up the gallery steps, while Gunther waited, a slumped shape on a horse.

Steve had a sharp look over his shoulder at the Kid, his face showing that he was of a mind to make the Kid stand outside. The Kid laughed again with his eyes, and Steve let him come. Inside, Steve made a motion toward the large room with the hewn rafters, saying, "Wait there."

"*Gracias*," said the Kid.

Steve went shouting about the house, his voice reaching to its far corners, and presently left the building, evidently for a look in the patio. He returned shortly to thrust his head into the doorway of the huge room. "Outside, you!" he ordered, and the Kid came to the gallery and found Gunther still sitting his saddle, but three people stood now in the yard. They were Rex Willard and Corinna and a stranger to the Beavertail, a tall man, ample of nose. They had about them an air of animosity that would have pierced a thinner skin than the Kid's, an animosity that needled the sunshine and left a stark hollowness to the silence.

Willard stared at the Kid and said, "For unmitigated temerity, this tops everything!"

The Kid shrugged and did then a strange thing. He looked toward the upper hills where the sky showed serene above the lifting pine, hunched his shoulders in a queer gesture and went at once to his horse and unlashed his slicker from behind the saddle. He donned the garment, buttoning it loosely around him, then stepped up to the saddle. From this perch, he said, "*Senor* Willard, do you weesh to return with me?"

Willard made no answer, turning instead to the tall stranger. Color spotted the sallow cheeks of Willard and anger made his voice harshly brittle. "Here is a sample of their boldness, Feathergill. The whole thing is

157

most obvious. I'm being given this chance to surrender to the very man who intended to lynch me! If I refuse, they can report to county law that I defied a deputy. That will be their excuse to attack Warbonnet."

Corinna looked about. "Where's Hap, Rex? He should be in on this."

Willard said, "He saddled up for himself and your dad about an hour ago. They've gone riding somewhere."

Gunther said stolidly, "A man got killed. We got a right to see justice done."

The Kid made the impatient shrug of one wishing to be done with a trivial matter. "Will you come, *Senor* Willard?"

Steve looked inquiringly at the Willards. "Shall I run 'em down the road, boss?"

Feathergill said then, "Now is the time to tell them." He lifted his glance to Gunther and said, "I'm Sam Feathergill," and showed his badge.

Gunther shook his shaggy head and said bitterly, "The best law for the richest man."

"No," Feathergill said and took a spread-legged stand, his thumbs hooked in his belt. "That isn't why I'm here. Mr. Willard sent for me, yes. But only to conduct a land opening. Warbonnet goes to the settlers."

Gunther said, "Lies, lies!"

"You'll have to believe it," Feathergill said.

"Warbonnet was never filed upon, and Mr. Willard has known that. He's also known that it's too big a ranch for the kind of cattle raising he and Mrs. Willard plan. Several weeks ago, he wrote Washington about the matter and asked that a marshal be sent out. While he was waiting, he had surveyors sent in who parceled out Warbonnet in quarter sections. A hundred and sixty acres will make a nice single-family farm in a valley as fertile as this one. Ride around and you'll find the surveyors' stakes all set."

Gunther looked like a man dealt a heavy blow. "Those strangers who come asking the way to Warbonnet? They were surveyors — not hired gunmen?"

"I've told you the place has been marked off into homesteads. I'm opening it up for settlement tomorrow noon. Mr. Willard hopes to claim one of those homesteads for himself."

"The best one," Gunther guessed. "This one where the buildings stand."

The edge of Feathergill's temper showed. "You blind, stubborn fool, can't you see he could have filed on this one any time and let the rest of you have what's left? If I'd been in his boots, I'd have done it. But he insists on taking the same chance as any other settler. The first plan was to have lots drawn. But some of you would grumble that the game was rigged. Now there's to be a land rush. A rip-snortin' old-fashioned land rush. You can carry that word back to town."

But still Gunther was unconvinced, and he shook his great shaggy head again. "A rich man doesn't give away what he wants for himself."

Willard stepped toward Gunther's horse and stood looking up. "See here, Gunther, what other way could I have found to give the lie to all that Mace Stroud has told you and your kind?"

Gunther said, "Tomorrow noon." He whispered it and was a man lost in amazement.

"Tomorrow noon," Feathergill said. "Will you carry the word?"

Gunther said to nobody, "I think we've been made big fools of."

Feathergill looked at the Kid, who sat his saddle unmoved by any of this. Feathergill said, "Ride out, you. If you're still around when I get my hands washed of this, I'll find something to hang onto you. Do you savvy?"

"*Si*," said the Kid, showing no real interest.

Steve stepped up to his saddle, a frankly disappointed man. "Come on, you two."

The three took to the road then, the Kid as imperturbable as ever, his dark eyes laughing their own secret laughter, and Gunther looking like a man whose convictions had at last been shaken. They came down through the timber to the gate, where the Kid was given his gun. They rode in silence to the south until Gunther began singing in a thunderous, unmusical voice, and when they neared the tent city at dusk, Gunther said, "I got to go spread the news. I got to tell everybody!"

"*Si,*" said the Kid, showing no real interest.

Gunther looked at him, his bovine eyes softening with something that was akin to pity. "You could get a farm, too."

"Ees not for me," said the Kid and laughed at Gunther with his eyes.

The Kid rode on alone then, lithe and dark and deadly, and found his way into Sawtelle and put up his horse and came to Pearl's Palace, still wearing the slicker. He climbed to Pearl's quarters and knocked upon the door; when Pearl bade him enter, he stepped quietly into that draped room with the canopied bed.

Pearl sat by the window, keeping the lamps unlighted. He said, with a trace of petulance, "I wondered what was delaying you."

The Kid unbuttoned the slicker and likewise unbuttoned his shirt and thrust a brown hand inside the shirt and tugged mightily. He brought out a tightly rolled canvas and dropped this at Pearl's feet with a fine Latin flourish. "Five minutes I am alone in the *hacienda*," he said. "Ees enough to cut the picture from the frame."

For a moment Pearl looked up at him, not believing, his round oily face vacuous with astonishment, and then Pearl came out of his chair and sprawled on the floor on his hands and knees, frantically smoothing the canvas. He spread it open and hovered over it, staring for a long while in silence. He came to a stand then and stood looking down at the canvas, his mouth working and his hands trembling. He began to laugh; his laughter was shrill and wild; it grew in intensity until it filled the room and made the room hideous.

The Kid waited until the laughter had died and then said patiently, "The *dinero* which you promised — ?"

Pearl looked at him as though he had forgotten the Kid's existence and just now discovered it. "Yes, the money," Pearl said. "You shall have it. And Sawtelle shall have such a night as it has never known."

The Peso Kid nodded. "That is true, I theenk. Ees big news tonight, *senor*, but not all of it ees good."

Deep dark came and the excitement with it, washing through Sawtelle in steady waves as

162

the word went from mouth to mouth and the settlers poured into town from the tent city and hammered the boardwalks with their boots.

Land rush!

That was the magic key to turbulence, the word that lifted in the night; and there was talk and speculation and men surging from place to place, blind and aimless in their excitement, and men huddling in tight knots in the shadows of the cottonwoods and the yellow splashings of light. There were dealings in horses, and any man with a fast mount could have put his own price on it. There was din and confusion and a high, constant fever; there was hope and fear and skepticism, with Gunther moving everywhere, Gunther telling his tale over and over.

And a man named Mace Stroud was not to be found on the street tonight; and a man named Larry Madden had rendezvous at Summit House.

In Pearl's Palace the lights blazed brightly, the smoke eddying to the ceiling; for the place was jammed from wall to wall and men banked deep at the bar where all the barkeeps sweated. There were free drinks tonight, and all a man had to do to earn his was to make his sneer at the picture above the bar. It hung in an improvised frame, and Tucker Ordway's likeness scowled down upon the revelers, the drink cadgers and the stray riders and the skeptical ones who lifted their insulting toasts to the painting. And upon all this Cibo Pearl beamed, strutting through the crowd. For if Mace Stroud was smarting in defeat tonight, Cibo Pearl was tasting his own kind of glory.

"He is dead, my friends, and there is nothing to fear!" he shouted. "Do you think there would be any land rush if Tucker Ordway were alive?"

Reva sang her songs, the crowd milling about her, drowning her out with their clamor; and the professor's piano became frenzied, catching the spirit of the night.

At a corner table Ames Luddington sat, nursing a cigar in remote loneliness, for no man had the patience for poker tonight. He watched the crowd and studied the picture above the bar and sometimes he smiled, but often his long, strong face was somber with his thinking. Reva came to his table between songs, choosing it because it was the farthest from the confusion, and sat there tired and silent. Cibo Pearl came also and presently fell to talking with Luddington. . . .

A percentage girl climbed to the bar, stripped off a garter and hung it over a corner of the picture to the raucous applause of the revelers. Another, inspired by the first one's show, also scrambled to the bar, a dozen hands helping her; and once standing, she pinned her garter to the picture in such a way that it appeared to be a ring in Ordway's nose. Laughter swept upward, none so great as Cibo Pearl's; and the barkeeps sweated on, the place rocking and roaring with sound. . . .

Thus it was that the long evening passed until the tent city people, realizing that a man must be fresh to ride for high stakes, drifted one by one from the town, and the boardwalks grew less thunderous and the revelers staggered from Pearl's Palace until the last of them was gone. The lights of the saloon blinked out, and silence and darkness at long last began to claim the town. The barkeeps had cleared the empty bottles from behind Pearl's bar; the swamper was showing himself from wherever he hid by day. On the edge of a boardwalk a Rafter-S cowboy sat hunched, nursing a scalp that had been laid open by the barrel of the Peso Kid's gun when some loyalty of cowman to cowman had made this one strike at a drunk who'd tossed a whiskey glass at Tucker Ordway's picture.

The cottonwoods whispered one to another, and the breeze stirred up a dust devil which went whirling down the street, catching up scraps of paper. A gaunt, gray tomcat emerged from the shadows beside the mercantile and boldly crossed the deserted street, and full hush held sway in Sawtelle.

13. Sixes at Summit House

Madden had come out of Doc Stone's that morning with his side newly bandaged and the damage from Stroud's fists tended to. But strong in his consciousness was an admonishment of Stone's that was like salt to his wounds.

"For all I care, you can beat Mace Stroud every day of his life," Stone had said. "He'd only be getting what's coming to him. But you'd better ask yourself what nursing a grudge is going to do to *you*. I saw the last of that fracas. Some men fight for fun and some fight for profit. With you, there's a devil digging inside. How long are you going to go snarling at the world like a rabid dog?"

"Look," Madden had said, "is that any of your damned business?"

He came back up the boardwalk to find Stroud standing in the doorway of his office, his huge arms hanging limp and his whole being slumped, his broken mouth grimacing at

167

Madden. Stroud glared stolidly at Madden, hating him with his eyes; but neither man spoke, and Madden thought: *Next time it will be guns.* He went on past, exposing his back to Stroud and chancing this show of contempt on the uncertain belief that Stroud hadn't yet the spirit to make a try at him.

He saw men in doorways, and no one of them spoke; he had awed them with his show of force, winning neither their respect nor their enthusiasm. A gray depression settled on him and it was his thought that he was little better than a liquored Indian letting his savagery loose and taking pride in such a brutal show.

Abreast of the mercantile, he found a man with the red-veined face and lackluster eyes of a confirmed drinker, and this man drew back and looked as though he were about to run. That was when Madden recognized him as Medwick, the coroner. He stopped Medwick by pinning a hard glance on the man, and he said, "Your patient is waiting. Go patch him up. And that will be your last job in Sawtelle. I'll be back here tonight or tomorrow. Don't let me find you in town."

Medwick made no answer; and Madden, looking into Medwick's eyes, saw there the man's terror and the man's surrender; and he knew that this one was through, just as Jess

168

Barker was through. He thought of that farce of an inquest and felt good.

He went to the livery stable and got his horse and rode out of the west end of Sawtelle's street.

He had that rendezvous with Tuck Ordway at Summit House, and he rode with the bitter knowledge that the fight with Stroud might stiffen him up, stealing from him the edge of resiliency he'd need when he faced Ordway at sundown. He flexed his right hand as he rode along, sometimes wrapping the reins around the saddlehorn so that he might massage his right hand with his left. He grew concerned about his hand, wondering if he'd thrown away a victory over Ordway to gain one over Stroud, and he saw the irony in this and laughed his silent laughter.

The stage road took him westward across meadowlands that lay like green carpeting before the hills, and by high noon he was climbing and could look back down upon Sawtelle and the gray blur of tents beyond the town. The day was good, warm enough, with no oppression to its heat, and the sky was a wide cloudlessness toward which Madden climbed. Soon the hills were crowding the road; and when he attained the first crest, he turned northward and began riding the ridges. Thus, having chosen this high route, he missed

169

meeting the Peso Kid and Gunther on their return from Warbonnet.

He offsaddled after an hour, resting himself, resting his horse; but he walked about
during part of this period, moving his arms
and shoulders like a boxer and opening and
closing his hands. He thought: *Tomorrow I'll
be like a board!* and was glad for that edge of
time.

He began riding again, mindful that the sun
made westing; he found the silence of the hills
a balm, and these bare wind-swept ridges gave
him a feeling of aloneness that turned his
thinking calm. Sometimes he had to drop
down into ravines between the ridges, finding
in them lost mountain meadows, and often he
forded the tiny creeks that moved tumul-
tuously downward to the floor of the Beavertail. He began looking at the sun more often,
conscious of time. Then he came into timber
and worked his way down through this timber
until he reached the old stage road and followed it into a broken expanse where only
stumps stood.

Here, in this clearing, was Summit House.
Shadows lay now before the large two-story
structure, and in the darkened doorway Hap
Sutton sat alone.

Madden looked at once for Sutton's horse
and another's; and not seeing them, he sup-

posed that Sutton had used the stable out back. He looked toward the open doorway behind Sutton and was instantly wary and then was ashamed. No man had ever challenged Tuck Ordway's courage; no man had ever accused him of ambush. Remembering this, he was left with only one interpretation for Sutton's being alone; and he swung down from his saddle and said, "So it was only talk, eh?"

Sutton said, "He's inside. Waiting."

"Out here should do," Madden said and gestured toward the stumpy openness.

Sutton squinted up at Madden's battered face and asked, irrelevantly, "Who marked you?"

"Stroud. I'm the one that walked away."

Sutton shook his head. "When you going to choose one side of the fence or the other?"

Madden said, "I'm here to make a fight, not to make talk."

Sutton shrugged. "Tuck wants it this way: you go in the front door, he goes in the back. When you find each other, you start shooting. That okay?"

Again there came that sense of wariness, and Madden looked at this man sharply. Texas had weathered that face, and the marching Montana years had put lines in it, but there was no guile in Sutton; there had never been. Madden thought: *It will be darker than the inside of a boot in there*, and he remembered that Ordway had specified sundown. There was something theatrical about Ordway's wish that irritated Madden, and he said, "What kind of fool play is this?"

"You don't have to do it."

Madden said, "Let's get it over with."

Sutton stood up. "You still want to go through with this?" he asked, and Madden made an impatient gesture with his hand. Sutton raised his voice. "He's coming in now, Tuck." And he stepped away from the door, making room for Madden.

All the waiting years rose then and rushed at Madden, the piled-up yesterdays, the accumulated hours between the one when smoke had risen from Circle M and this moment when he stepped toward Tucker Ordway; the far trails and the far horizons once forgotten came again to him, and the deep nights that had lain outside lonely campfire rims, and the long days on other ranges, the towns that were all alike and the passing faces that were never familiar. All of the great ragged circle came now to its finish.

"Ordway," he shouted. "I've got a gun in my hand."

But he had a moment to remember Doc Stone and Reva and the tasteless aftermath of this morning's fight, and in that moment he wondered how far his trail might take him if this were not the end of it. The sting of the whip was long since gone, only the marks remaining. He wondered then if there might be a night when he would look at himself in some remote bar mirror and see himself as the Peso Kid, with only this one difference: he hadn't taken pay for a killing. A word from Ordway might have stopped him then; but Summit House held silent, and he stepped through the doorway.

There was nothing here but growing darkness, thicker than the shadows outside, that and the smell of ancient dust and a scurrying that might have been a rat's. To his right, the great cobweb-festooned bar loomed, running the length of the wall, and he wondered: *Behind that?* and tilted his gun toward the bar and stood waiting. Somewhere the floor creaked to the weight of a boot; and Madden instantly turned, probing the shadows and damning Ordway's whim that had made of this a duel in darkness.

He called up all his memory of the place, wishing now that he'd taken a good look around that day he'd been here with Reva. Back yonder, somewhere, was the stairway to the second floor; and back there, too, were rooms once used for storage. Madden laid his gun carefully on the floor and seated himself soundlessly and tugged off his boots. He picked up the gun and stood erect and began moving to the rear of the building, mindful of the crippled tables and chairs strewn about; and he heard then a soft padding movement and tried to locate it. He had to smile, knowing now that Ordway, too, had removed his boots.

When he had groped his way to the rear, he found a door giving into one of the storage rooms. He put his hand to this door and let it swing inward. The hinges made a great shrieking in the heavy silence; and he at once pressed close to the wall, listening. The last light shafted through a rear window into the room; and when he risked a look, he saw that the room was empty. Still, he gave its shadowy corners careful consideration, then turned to the next room.

His skin was beginning to crawl, and he felt sweat at his armpits and sweat in his eyes, and the place choked him, layered as it was with all the ancient odors of abandonment. He found the second room empty and the third, but he went through the same careful ritual of inspection in each one, then began groping along the rear wall. He came upon the doorway by which Ordway had entered the building, and he heard then a creak on the stairs and was startled to find that the stairs were squarely before him.

Anger took hold of him, and he shouted, "Ordway! Come down from there!"

He got no answer, and he supposed that Ordway was waiting at the head of the stairs, waiting for him to make the ascent. He stepped into the stairwell and pressed hard against its wall and went up the steps. They protested his weight, and he had a panicky moment, fearing Ordway's gunfire. He ascended swiftly then, knowing that Ordway was expecting him and knowing, too, that wariness couldn't serve him any longer. He got to the upper hall, breathing hard, and still the silence of Summit House held tight.

There were no windows along this hallway. Doors gave from the corridor into rooms where travelers had once slept. Madden wondered if Ordway had taken to one of these rooms and if he must now hunt the man down. He moved from the stairway to one of the walls and felt along it for a door, being infinitely careful about this; and Ordway said then, out of the darkness, "I'm here, Madden."

Madden stiffened but was suddenly done with fear, done with waiting. He found it hard to orient Ordway's voice, but he knew that the man must be down the hallway. He fired in that direction, closing his eyes briefly to keep from being blinded by his own gunflash. Then Ordway fired, too; the crash of the gun thunderous in this narrow place, the gunflame a great orange slash in the dark. Ordway's bullet thunked into a far wall; and Madden at once fired a second shot, knowing now where Ordway stood, for he'd glimpsed him in the gunflame.

He heard Ordway fall; the man lay still, but Madden waited out one minute after another in the stifling dark until Sutton's voice rose from below, crying, "Tuck? Tuck? Is it over?"

Madden shouted, "Come up here!" and moved along the wall, groping till he found where Ordway lay. Oddly, there was nothing for him in this moment but curiosity. He felt of the man; Ordway lay face down on the planking. He risked a match and saw blood on Ordway's right shoulder. Ordway raised his face to him in the match's flare, then slumped into complete unconsciousness.

The match burned down to Madden's fingers, and he dropped it and whispered aloud, "Blind! Blind as a bat!"

Sutton came fumbling up the stairs. "Where the devil are you?"

Madden said, "Here. Come give me a hand. He's hurt, but he's not dead."

Together they lifted Ordway and got him

along the hall and down the stairs. The descent was difficult, and then they had to grope with their burden across the barroom and out through the door, and here they laid Ordway upon the ground.

Madden said, "Just a minute," and went back in after his boots. He found them and stomped into them and came outside again to find that Sutton had fetched one of the saddle blankets from the stable and was rolling Ordway onto it. Madden helped him, then stood watching while Sutton tore away Ordway's shirt and had a look at the wound.

"Not too bad," Sutton said. "Shock knocked him out." He at once got out of his vest and shirt and began tearing strips from his undershirt to make a pad and tie. When this was done to his satisfaction, he stood up.

Madden said then, "How long has he been blind, Hap?"

"Two-three years. His eyes have been going gradually. He's still got some sight. Not much."

Anger rose in Madden. "You could have told me!"

"And had you make talk about it in Sawtelle where Stroud and Pearl would hear? How could I be sure how you stood? And how long do you think Stroud would hold off if he knew Tuck couldn't see worth a damn?"

Madden remembered his first visit to Doc Stone's and the medico's telling him to forget his feud or he would be sorry, and he remembered, too, that Stone had been at Warbonnet just yesterday. Now he understood why. He looked at Sutton and said, "At least you could have kept him from this fight."

Sutton met his stare and anger came into Sutton's own voice. "What in hell else did he have left but his pride? Will you tell me that? What in hell else was there?"

"Yes," Madden said. "That's right."

"That's why he wanted it this way," Sutton said and gestured toward the house. "You and him in darkness, feeling your way toward each other. That made it fair enough, didn't it? You blind and him blind."

"Fair enough," Madden said and found that the backwash of released tension had made his knees unsteady.

Sutton walked to the doorway and sat down in it, suddenly a tired old man. He shaped up a cigarette and drew upon it, and he said then, "I'm going to make a speech."

Madden said, "Make it."

"Every man is a little crazy on some one thing. Maybe he shows it — maybe he doesn't. Besides Warbonnet, the only thing that ever meant a damn to Tuck Ordway was that girl of his. Some day he was going to lose

178

her; he knew that, but he didn't like thinking about it. The only man hereabouts she ever took a shine to was you. But you never showed yourself at Warbonnet; you were too high and mighty for that. She had to sneak away to Circle M to see you. Tuck got wise to that. The whole thing had a smell to it, if you stop to remember about that one crazy spot in Tuck."

Madden said, "I'd have come to Warbonnet when I had a herd big enough to match Warbonnet's."

Sutton spurted smoke through his nostrils. "How was Tuck to know that? He only knew that Corry was eating her heart out one year after another and sneaking off to see you. So Tuck jumped you that day in Sawtelle and told you to leave her alone. You got mouthy, and that was when he laid his whip on you. Okay, son. He was wrong — dead wrong. But you collected back for that tonight. I tried to tell you you'd be sorry when you did. Now you've found out."

Madden said, "He must have still had some hate in him. He didn't need to ask me in yesterday and call for this show."

Sutton made a spreading gesture with his hands. "He knew Warbonnet was being pushed by enemies. He gave you your chance to say whether you were one of them. You

179

spoke your piece. There ain't much Tuck has been able to do lately. I think he figgered it a fair risk if coming here lifted one enemy off Warbonnet's back."

He stood up and crossed to where Ordway lay and knelt down beside him and put his ear to Ordway's chest, then listened to Ordway's breathing. "He's sleeping now," Sutton said. "I'll let him sleep himself out."

Madden said, "You may need help getting him back to Warbonnet."

Sutton said, "I think you'd better be riding. I don't reckon he'd want that help from you."

"No," Madden said, "he wouldn't." He crossed to his waiting horse and lifted himself to the leather and reined among the stumps to the old stage road.

14. The Dark Hours

In the silence that laid hold on Pearl's Palace, the echoing silence that made strange aftermath to the riotous night, only the swamper worked, an obscure, bent figure in the vastness of the empty barroom. All the cutglass-festooned lamps had been extinguished but one; the swamper's shadow was a dancing, grotesque thing. The professor had gone home and so had the barkeeps and the housemen, and Pearl was overhead in his draped room. Only Reva sat at a table, her fatigue showing in her face, her eyes still with deep thinking. Outside, the town lay quiet, so quiet as to have no heartbeat at all. The swamper's mop made hard, rasping sounds against the floor; the swamper's breathing was asthmatic and heavy.

Reva looked at him and thought: *Poor tired old man,* pitying him at first and then feeling a strange kinship which she searched to its core. Then she thought: *Why, he belongs to Cibo, too, just like me and the professor and all the others!* She found this reflection both comforting

and discomforting; it took away her aloneness, but it held in it the rub of fetters and the
full, bitter realization of what the piled-up
years could do to her.

She often stayed here alone after her night's
work was done, delaying the moment when
she needs must go upstairs. She had found
that in these dark hours when the piano stood
mute and the last glass empty she could make
a strange sort of peace with herself and her
way of life; it was like the aloneness of riding
the wide valley on her day off. But tonight being here brought no balm to her, and she wondered about this, all her thinking gray and
weary and troublesome.

She looked up at Tucker Ordway's picture.
The garter still hung from the painted nose;
above it the implacable eyes looked out defi-
antly; the hard jaw seemed steeled against the
insult. Someone had hurled a whiskey glass at
the picture and gouged the canvas, but Pearl
had put a stop to that, not wanting the painting irreparably damaged. Reva remembered
that and the whole hideous evening, and she
thought of the evenings like it that were to follow.

She came out of her chair then and moved
toward the bar and stood looking up at the
picture, not seeing it really. She felt ill and
wanted to be out in the night and thought of

walking. But she stood riveted here, held somehow by that picture, and held, also, by all her thoughts.

Once there'd been a man . . .

Yes, once there'd been a man, and he'd worn black as Cibo Pearl did, but he'd been a tall man with a guileful tongue and a smile to charm the angels. Sometimes she found it hard to remember the man's face, but always she remembered his smile. Somewhere she'd heard in recent years that he was dead, just as the baby was dead. He'd never even seen the child, and she wondered if he had if that might have made a difference. She seldom let herself think of the baby; for whenever she did, she felt the need to run when there was nowhere to run.

That was how it had all begun, and she had long since lost count of the towns she'd known and the places like this one with sawdust on the planking and a glittering battalion of bottles doubled in a bar mirror and the tuneless, cigarette-scarred piano and the death-faced housemen with their green visors and their soulless skill.

There had been other men, too, some of them lean, some of them fat, some kind in their fashion, some cruel. She looked back at them across the years; she looked at all the places she'd known, and she searched that long, long trail, trying to find some little good she'd done along it; and she remembered Madden and her seeing him to Summit House and bandaging his wound.

She weighed this against all the rest and found it a small thing, scarcely counting, and she shook her head and was very tired.

The swamper came toward her, collecting the spittoons. She made room for him, and he gave her a long, searching look and asked, "Can I get you something, ma'am?"

"No, thanks."

He shuffled toward the rear of the room with an armload of spittoons, and the back door banged as he took them into the alley. She was truly alone now, and suddenly she knew what it was she must do and was frightened with the knowledge. And because she made no false estimate of her courage, she went at her work quickly while her will was strong, climbing to the top of the bar and reaching for Tucker Ordway's picture. The wire suspending it proved stubborn, and she had to wrestle mightily to free it. She almost quailed then. But the picture came loose, and she got it laid on the bar, and she stepped down to the floor and stood breathing heavily.

On a shelf behind the bar she found many things — a bung-starter, a sawed-off shotgun laid convenient to the barkeep's hand, a litter of miscellaneous objects that had found their way to the shelf. Among these was a butcher knife. She took this and resolutely cut Ordway's picture from its frame. Her fingers became frantic; her great desire was to get this done before she could think what she was doing, think of the consequences. For she wanted that picture destroyed so there could be no other night like this one, and she tried ripping the canvas. With the knife, she at last succeeded in slashing the picture across.

Now she methodically began hacking the canvas into smaller strips. She worked at this in a frenzy, sometimes glancing toward the rear door where the swamper must soon appear. She made shreds of each strip, tossing them away when she was sure they were ruined beyond repair. She was at this when she felt eyes upon her and looked up to see Cibo Pearl standing at the head of the stairs before the door of his quarters.

"I wondered, my dear, what was keeping you," he said.

Then it was he realized what she'd been doing, for his look turned blank with surprise, and then the anger came into his little eyes and his face became something molded from putty, gray and formless and absurd. His mouth worked, but no words came from him; the sound was an animal's.

Terror overcame Reva, and she wanted to turn and run, but at first her legs refused to obey her. Then she darted toward the bat-wings, and she heard Pearl's voice lift behind her, shrill and maniacal with rage. Something smote her in the small of her back, and a gun made a quick, waspish sound. The shot flung her around; she reached out blindly and clutched at the end of the bar for support and clung there, looking up. And now, because she knew she was dying, her fear left her; her face was serene and she was faintly smiling.

She could see Pearl up there at the head of the stairs, his body seemingly hunched and shrunken, a smoking derringer in his hand. Someone made a wild exclamation of shocked astonishment, and she saw the swamper then, standing in the opened rear doorway below Pearl. The swamper looked full at Reva, then lifted his startled face toward Pearl. Pearl instinctively tilted the gun, but the swamper was gone, bolting into the night. Pearl looked down at the gun in his hand, and suddenly his face held the fearful awareness of a man who has too late learned that his temper has plunged him into disaster.

Then Pearl, too, was bolting, scurrying back into his room, a man ridden by a full realization that he had at last gone too far. And knowing this, Reva still smiled and smiling slipped gently down to the sawdust to lie there like a crumpled flower. . . .

Madden came riding in at this past-midnight hour, worn from the long trail back from Summit House and grim with the knowledge he had gained at that high hill rendezvous. He put up his saddler and felt his weariness then, and his hunger, but as he came along the deserted boardwalk, he saw no restaurant with a light showing and was not too disappointed. He had a need that was greater than that for food, and he went at once to the Ogallala House and climbed the stairs and found his way to Ames Luddington's room.

He expected Luddington would be in bed, but his business with Luddington wouldn't keep, not in his present mood; and he was astonished when Luddington, admitting him, proved to be fully clothed. The lamp wasn't lighted, and the man had moved the one chair to the window; by these tokens Madden judged that Luddington had kept awake by watching the street.

Luddington said petulantly, "Where in the name of sense have you been?"

There was about him an intense nervousness that made him at once begin pacing, his strong face worried and grim. He turned and faced Madden, spreading his hands apart and not waiting an answer as he said, "You know, don't you, that the whole thing has blown up in our faces."

Madden said, "I've been out of town."

Luddington sat down on the bed and combed his hair with his fingers. "I've been stupid," he muttered. "Plain stupid. You'll remember that I had a marshal coming. There was one thing I overlooked; it never occurred to me to check in Washington and see if anyone else had made the same arrangement. But Rex Willard had done just that. By mail, I guess. His marshal's at Warbonnet right now — a man named Sam Feathergill."

Madden's interest sharpened. "A tall man, big-nosed?" he asked, remembering the traveler he'd met on the trail from Warbonnet.

Luddington nodded. "That's the way he's been described."

Madden said, "It doesn't matter."

Luddington turned a fierce look upon him. "It matters very much! Do you recall my telling you that strangers had showed up recently, asking the way to Warbonnet? Stroud was afraid they might be hired gunhands; actually they were government surveyors Willard brought in to mark off Warbonnet into quarter sections. Now the whole place is to be thrown open to entry tomorrow. Every inch of it. The idealistic damned fool!"

Madden said, "I told you it doesn't matter!"

Luddington got up from the bed and began pacing again. "It's going to be handled like a small scale Cherokee Strip opening. Any qualified man can register and then run for it and plant his stake. Those surveyors have been posted out in the valley to keep sooners from sneaking in tonight or tomorrow morning. Willard's racing, too; he wants the quarter section where the ranch buildings stand. Do you understand, Larry? He could have filed on that himself and thrown open the rest of it, if he'd wished. But he's giving the lie to Stroud's defamations by taking the same chance as anyone else."

"Let him have it."

"Look," Luddington said, "you think me a city man with no understanding of this business. Have you forgotten that I ranch in Nevada? I've seen Warbonnet from this side of the wire. Homestead that quarter section where the buildings stand, and you've got the sweetest small ranch in Montana. Buildings already up. Grass for all the blooded stock you'd want to raise. Summer pasture in the hills. Water. Everything. I saw that at once. And that was to be Larry Madden's quarter section when *my* marshal got here!"

Madden said wearily, "You had it all wrong, Ames. From the first. I wanted Tuck Ordway's hide, not his house. Once I figured to break him first, but not for my own gain. But that's over and done with, too. He's blind, Ames, blind."

Luddington appeared not to hear. "We've still got a chance, Larry," he insisted, his face eager and thoughtful. "Two things could swamp that race — men and horses. Half of the entrymen will be riding old crowbaits that will fall apart at the end of the first mile. A lot of them were trying to buy better horses tonight, but most of that was wishful thinking; they couldn't afford a real horse. You've got the money, Larry. You can buy up every worthwhile horse tomorrow morning. Then you'll need men to ride them — the kind of men who'll do what they're told. Stroud's got men — so has Pearl."

Madden said drily, "I don't think Stroud would want to string along with me."

Luddington made an impatient gesture. "Yes, I heard what you did to Stroud this morning. Make your peace with him! Wave a profit under his nose! Tell him that if you can get the buildings, he can have Warbonnet's next best piece of land. Put twenty men on twenty good horses, and you'll sleep in Tucker Ordway's bed tomorrow night!"

Madden was suddenly tired of all this, yet he'd never been further from anger; he was beyond anger and knew only a great, deep sickness. He reached and got his hand on Luddington's shoulder, stopping the man's pacing, and he said, "I think, Ames, that you'd better catch the next stagecoach out and head back to Frisco. Whatever I owe you, you'll get. But we're through, mister."

Luddington brushed his hand away. "Don't you go being a damned fool, too! What sense was there in coming back if you only lined your pocket with Ordway's scalp? I've seen that from the first."

Madden said, "Ever since we met here in Sawtelle, you've had one set of notions and I've had another. I'm not riding in that race. I'm riding out of here tonight. Do you understand? The game's over."

Luddington's eyes met Madden's, and in Luddington a bitter judgment showed plain. "You mean that, don't you, Larry?"

"I mean it."

"Very well. From now on, I'm on my own," Luddington said. "Throw away your chance if you like, but I'm riding for a homestead. The one you're too big a fool to want."

Madden said, "Ride and be damned," and turned on his heel and left the room.

He came along the hall and fumbled for his

own door and let himself in. He moved to the window and stood looking out, his thoughts chaotic, his body tired. All that Stroud's fists had done lay like a weight on him. He looked toward the bed and longed to be in it. He said aloud, "Oh, hell!" and thought of riding at once, leaving all this behind him; and he heard then the footsteps in the hall and the knock at the door.

His first thought was that it was Luddington come to make some sort of peace, and he said wearily, "Come in," and found Doc Stone in the doorway.

Stone said breathlessly, "There's a girl dying over at my house. She keeps calling for you. I've been here twice now. Will you come?"

"Reva!" Madden said, not knowing how he knew.

Stone nodded. "Better hurry it."

"I'll come," Madden said and moved at once toward the door.

15. To the Swift

A man sat hunched on the steps of Doc Stone's house as the medico and Madden came through the gate, and Madden recognized him vaguely as a swamper from Pearl's Palace. The man had the look of one who waited because there was nothing else to do, nowhere else to go; he looked old and used up and inadequate. Stone greeted him with a grunt and led the way at once into the house and to a bedroom giving off his office. Reva lay in the bed, and Stone shoved Madden toward her and said, "I fetched him."

Reva smiled. "Hello, Larry."

Only a dim lamp burned here, and in its light Reva looked younger and at peace with herself; her black curls lay fanned out against the pillow, and she might have been a little girl making a great show of being sick, pleased with the small attentions and manifested concern of her elders. She was in pain, but she hid the pain, and Madden was not fooled.

He stepped to the edge of the bed and stood looking down at her, his fists bunched. "Who did this to you, Reva?" he demanded.

Reva said, "Please sit down, Larry. I have things I must tell you."

On the way over, Stone had mumbled something about a gunshot wound, and Madden looked now at the doctor, asking Stone with his eyes whether it was all right for her to talk. Stone made a hunching movement with his shoulders, saying nothing, yet making an eloquent answer: *It doesn't matter. Not any more.*

Madden lowered himself to a chair, his anger beating in his temples. His great desire was to wrest the truth from her, to find out who'd felled her, but he wanted also to bring her some kind of comfort, so he said, "It's all over between me and Ordway. We had our showdown yesterday. He's alive. Why wasn't I told that he was blind?"

Reva said, "What then, Larry? You'd have ridden away feeling defeated and still carrying your hate with you. I think that now you will purge yourself. It shows in your eyes."

Pain moved in her, and her face suddenly twisted with it. She fought against this and controlled herself; she waved Doc Stone back from the bed to which he had instantly moved. She said, "I want to talk about Corinna and Rex, Larry."

Stone said irritably, "Let her have her

say," and left the room.

Madden looked at Reva and had a consciousness of sands running out and a feeling of helplessness which scared him. He said gently, "I'm listening."

Reva closed her eyes. "They have a dream, those two. Corry used to speak of it when we met. The day of the big ranch is done, Larry; you know that. It's to be blooded cattle instead of native stock, a few acres and controlled feeding rather than vast herds thrown carelessly through the hills. Tucker Ordway has lived in the past; Corry is looking to the future. All she and Rex want is a quarter section so they can run a small ranch the new way. That's why they're willing to let the rest of Warbonnet go."

Madden said, "I see. . . . "

"Rex will ride tomorrow, Larry, to stake out that quarter section where the buildings stand. He could have filed on that piece of range when he first came here. But tonight he has friends among the settlers because he didn't; they can't overlook such an act of faith. Those who once chased him are ashamed of themselves now. Rex is farsighted. He knows that if his dream comes true, he'll have those settlers for neighbors. That made their friendship important. He'll gain it tomorrow by taking his chances right along with them. But

there is more to it than that. Can you understand why a rich man might want, just once,
to earn something for himself with no odds in
his favor?"

Madden asked, "What's this to me?"

Reva opened her eyes. "Nothing really. But
I want you to ride in that race. Not for a piece
of land, but to watch Rex Willard's back."

Madden's lips thinned. "I think I've done
enough for him."

"No," Reva said, "you haven't. You're the
one who brought Ames Luddington here, and
Luddington is the man Rex will have to fear
most tomorrow."

Madden showed his surprise. "How do you
know about Luddington?"

"I told you once that Cibo talked in front of
me, Larry. Luddington came to the Palace
last night and laid out his cards, telling Cibo
who he was and why he was here. He wanted
to make a deal with Cibo to swamp the race tomorrow, for Luddington himself wants the
quarter section where Warbonnet's buildings
stand."

Madden asked quickly, "This happened
tonight? Early tonight?"

Reva tried to nod. "Cibo had begun to mis-
trust me, I think, for he took Luddington upstairs. But I heard enough at the table to know
that Luddington is sharpening his own axe."

Madden said slowly, "Yes, he's been sharpening it all along."

"I think I know men, Larry. Mace Stroud is the least dangerous of those who want Warbonnet. He's big-mouthed and wolf-brave but anyone can see him coming a mile off. Pearl is twice as smart and therefore twice as dangerous. Luddington is smarter than either of them, and Luddington is the kind to play the ends against the middle. Rex may stand a chance against Stroud or Cibo, but he'll need help with Luddington against him."

"I finished with Luddington tonight," Madden said. "I didn't know he'd already doublecrossed me. He said he was going to ride."

"And when you finished with him, you turned him loose against Rex. Isn't that so?"

Madden closed and opened his hands. "I hadn't thought of it that way."

"Will you ride, Larry?"

He said, "I won't promise. There is something that concerns me more than that race. Who shot you, Reva? Cibo? No, he wouldn't pull his house down over his head. Was it a stray bullet in a saloon brawl? I'll find out anyway."

"Don't try to. You'd trade one hate for another. You'd go looking for somebody else as you looked for Tucker Ordway. I want you free, Larry."

She fell silent then, and she was silent so long that he stirred himself, thinking she had slipped away. He was beat-out tired, and this room was too drowsy for him with its shaded lamp and soft shadows. He knew that death was here, but there was no reality to the knowledge. Then he looked at Reva and found her fighting pain again, and the reality rose up and crowded the room. He took her hand and asked urgently, "Shall I call Doc Stone?"

Her eyes told him no. Her spasm passed and she lay peacefully against the pillow, and she asked then, incongruously, "How old are you, Larry?"

"Twenty-eight."

She said, "Luddington told us tonight about your mine in Arizona. I want you to be richer than that; you were meant to ride with the sun in your face and your eyes smiling. How long has it been since you got up thinking it was a good day ahead? You've got all the years to come and all that a man could ask. Will you make it a good life for you, Larry?"

He said, "You want my promise, don't you? About Rex."

She smiled. "A promise would just be a chain. No, if you ride beside Rex tomorrow, it must be because you want to."

He puzzled over that, knowing that it was

very important that he understand her, and while he puzzled, she said very softly, "You're the man I should have met so long, long ago, Larry. Would you have been interested?"

"When you are well again, we'll ride out of here together," he said, and the lie tasted clean upon his lips.

She sighed; presently she seemed to sleep, but he felt the tremor in her hand. She clung to him and then her hand went still; and he came to a stand and looked down at her and was suddenly frantic, his raised voice fetching Stone.

The medico had his look and drew the blanket up over Reva's face and turned to Madden. "You'd better go now."

Madden came out of the house like a man sleep-walking and found the hunched figure of the swamper still on the steps. He knew now why this man had waited, and he said, "She's gone, friend."

The swamper thought about this and then gave his judgment. "She was different from most. She had something to her. Something solid."

Madden said then in sudden terrible understanding, "So it happened in Pearl's place. You saw it and fetched the doctor and the two of you carried her here, and then you waited. And now you don't dare go back because it was Cibo himself!"

The swamper said, "That's the size of it."

Madden dug into his pocket and found a gold piece. "Buy yourself a bed somewhere," he said as he passed over the coin. "This will be a safe town for you before the sun goes down again."

He went up the boardwalk with a single-mindedness that left him blind to the town. The edge of dawn was showing; this first light made of the buildings bleak, gray silhouettes, homely as sin and a scar upon nature. He came to Pearl's Palace and found its front open; and he strode into the silent, deserted, sawdust-strewn expanse of the barroom and went at once to the stairs and climbed to Pearl's quarters. He shouldered through the door recklessly, calling out Pearl's name and laying oaths to it, and the place echoed his voice, the echo mocking him. He looked at that canopied bed and strode to it and wrenched the canopy loose and flung the cloth across the floor. He came back downstairs and explored the farther recesses of the place and found Pearl nowhere.

He thought: *He's run already!* and he stood contemplating this thought until a measure of patience came back to him and his first heady anger gave way to one that was cold and calculating and relentless. Which trail? Which trail?

He was struck by another thought and went at once to the Ogallala and climbed to Luddington's room, remembering that Luddington had made himself Pearl's ally. He found the room empty and this puzzled him; he supposed Luddington would be getting his rest for the race. He walked to his own room and stood in it, his eyelids heavy and all his thinking clouded by weariness. He knew that he had to rest before he could go on with his hunting. He told himself he would lie down for only a few minutes, but first he propped the chair under the doorknob.

He stretched himself out upon the bed, not removing his boots, and all his weariness rolled over him in one vast wave, and he was carried out upon that wave to oblivion . . .

Sunlight lay in the room when he aroused, and he was at once conscious that it was mid-morning and that Sawtelle had never been so noisy at this hour. He got off the bed and found himself stiff from yesterday morning's fight, but not so stiff as he'd supposed he would be. He went to the window and had a look at the street and saw that it was jammed with vehicles and that saddlers stood at every hitchrail and men moved endlessly along the boardwalks, the babble of their voices lifting in a steady beat of sound. He washed his face in cold water and came down to the dining room and ate and asked of someone when the race would be run.

"High noon, mister."

He thought of Reva, dead in Doc Stone's house; he thought of Luddington who had sold him out and of Cibo Pearl who had shot a woman. Somewhere was the beginning of Pearl's trail, and he had wasted more time than he'd intended.

So thinking, he came out to the Ogallala's long gallery and found Rex Willard and Corinna standing there.

He went at once to the pair and said, "I know about Tuck Ordway. That's over and done with." He nodded at Willard. "Good luck when you ride."

Willard looked at him, his face warming to this first show of friendliness; and then Willard turned sober. "Thank you," he said. "But I've just learned that I won't be riding."

Madden said, "How's that?"

"Mace Stroud talked to Feathergill, the marshal, early this morning. Feathergill's taken some liberties in the way he's managing this opening, but he can't buck all the laws. Stroud claims that an entryman can't be one with a criminal charge against him. I'm still charged with murder, remember. I could go down to Yellow Lodge with you and clear myself, but there isn't time now. Feathergill understands that the charge was trumped-up, but he doesn't want to go interfering with county law. So I'm just not qualified."

Madden said, "And I ran Medwick out of town!" But he was thinking: *It took Luddington to think up this twist!* and he remembered the man's being absent from his room early this morning, and he remembered, too, what Reva had said about Luddington being the most dangerous.

Corinna said, "It doesn't matter. By law, a married woman is disqualified to file on a homestead unless her husband is in a penitentiary. But I'm riding in his place just the same. We'll take it to court afterwards, if we have to."

Madden thought of the wire-strung homesteads and the broken fields at this south end of the valley; and he thought, too, of all the men and all the vehicles that would be in the race, the frenzy of it and the rush of it; and he said, "Willard, you're not letting her do it! Warbonnet's got men, hasn't it?"

Willard shook his head. "I've been trying to talk her out of it. But most of our boys are riding to get homesteads for themselves. After tonight, we'd need no crew but Hap Sutton. I can't ask the crew to give up their own chances to make one for us."

Corinna said, "Hap's in town today, and we

could have him ride. But this race is to the swift and that means to the young. Either I ride, or we have no chance at all."

The silent laughter bubbled up in Madden, for he saw irony here. "They kept my name out of the inquest so they could hang the charge on you," he reminded Willard. "That leaves me clear. Corinna, you stay out of it. I'll ride. I know that an applicant has to swear he's not making an entry to give another person the benefit, but we'll wrangle that out with the law later."

Corinna raised her eyes to him, her hope in her face, and he had never seen her so beautiful. "Why, Larry? Why this for us?"

He had nothing with which to ward off her gratitude but gruffness, so he said brusquely, "Call it what you please," and turned and strode down off the gallery.

But now he was remembering Reva and the wisdom of Reva, for suddenly he knew what she had meant about a man riding with the sun in his face and his eyes smiling.

16. Tall Man Riding

Feathergill had set up a registry booth on the street, and here Madden was given a certificate to locate on land, a pointed wooden stake, and some instructions to which he listened with half an ear. Feathergill recognized him from that meeting in the Beavertail and pinned upon him a hard and thoughtful look but said no more than had to be said; Feathergill was showing a tired impatience, for he had had a morning of this, and the hour of the opening was drawing near.

Madden went then to the livery stable and got his horse and saw that the hostler had a sawed-off shotgun propped against the wall. The man looked as though he'd slept little. Horses had been at a premium these past eighteen hours, and some might have wanted one desperately enough to try stealing it.

Madden did his own saddling, being very careful about this, and led the mount out to the street. For a moment the thought of Cibo Pearl came back to him, so strong and crowding that it put an ache in his hands. Then he deliberately banished Pearl from his mind, knowing that the ride before him would call for all his thought and all his will.

He remembered Luddington, too, and supposed that Luddington was out there somewhere along the starting line, just north of the tent town. He rode to the line and found it a long, heaving, buckling row of men, scores of men, some on horseback and some in light rigs — spring wagons, sulkies, buckboards. Here and there the weathered tilts of covered wagons showed, and on the seat of at least one of these sat a woman, some settler's work-worn wife, out to see this thing through. Madden sensed how desperately these people wanted their prize, a chance at a home, a place to sink down roots, and suddenly he had a great and encompassing sympathy for all of them; he wished them well.

He looked along the line, wondering again about Luddington; dust cast a hazy pall, and the blended voices of men made a constant thunder, and then the silence came as though someone had signaled it. All of the waiting was done with, the waiting and the commotion that had come from men crowding for front places. The line seemed to settle and become frozen. For Sam Feathergill had ridden up and was sitting his saddle with his six-shooter lifted in his hand; and the sun stood at noon.

Feathergill's face was impassive; his hand lifted higher, and the gun spoke; and Warbonnet was now open to entry. It was done, as simply as this; and in Madden was the strange feeling that he could weep if he were to let himself.

The line broke with a concerted yell lifting; the dust at once began to boil; and Madden touched spurs to his mount. Just ahead of him, the wheels of a pair of wagons pressed too closely together locked, and the drivers went spilling, their hopes going down in the dust. But Madden wasn't in that mad melee. Wheeling his horse to the west, he went riding hard along the fringe of Sawtelle; and once clear of the town, he took to the stage road as he had yesterday morning when he'd gone to his rendezvous at Summit House.

He had put his own wisdom to the task at hand, giving it thought in the little time he'd had since he'd left Rex and Corinna Willard on the gallery of the Ogallala, and he had then chosen this longer way to reach Warbonnet. It had been his judgment that the race would belong to the canny as well as to the swift.

His horse was fresh enough to want to go, and he let it stretch out, coming thus across the meadowlands, with the hills bulking ahead of him and the sky the same wide cloudlessness of yesterday. His body was stiff, a constant reminder of his fight with Stroud. He wondered if this might count too heavily against him when his last edge was needed, and he fell to worrying about it.

When the hills began crowding the road, he pulled his mount down to a walk, knowing he must ration the horse's reserve as a careful man rations food on a long, lonely trail. At the first crest, where he turned northward to ride the ridges, he looked down upon Sawtelle and saw to the north of town a great chaos of dust where the boomers fought their way through the tangle of farms spreading across this end of the valley. He guessed that most of them would lose time there, a great deal of time, fighting the checkerboard pattern of fences and plowed fields, and upon this guess had rested his decision to take the hill route. He would have extra miles to ride, but he was gambling that those miles would not count so much against him as yonder first stretch was counting against those who'd faced directly northward.

On these high, wind-swept ridges, he again put the horse forward at a run, and when he came to where he'd offsaddled and rested the day before, he would have liked nothing better than to do so again. He made only this compromise: he let the horse go at a plodding walk for a while, and he thought then how convenient it would be if he had staked out a fresh horse here. This reminded him of Luddington's proposal that the race be swamped, and he wondered how Luddington fared down there in the valley's dust.

The ravines slowed him, but he took their slants recklessly until he felt that the horse was slowly giving out. He grew more careful of the horse then, choosing easy ascents but losing precious minutes. He had to command himself to patience; but when he again attained a ridge where he could see down into the valley, he found that the lifting dust was behind him, which meant that he must be ahead of the mass of settlers.

He rested himself and rested his horse for a minute and put his speculation upon the racers. Some others also had seen that the straight way was not the best way. Dust rose almost directly below him, he now discovered, and dust rose to the far side of the valley. Wary entrymen had chosen to skirt the base of the hills, avoiding the farmland barrier. Thus the van of the rush was a huge curve, stretching the width of the valley.

Far upon the valley's floor, ahead of the dust cloud, he made out minute figures which were men on horses, and he wondered about these, for they were not riders in a hurry. Then he remembered that Feathergill had stationed the surveyors to keep out sooners, those who might have started ahead of the signal gun, and he judged that the waiting horsemen, so tiny and toy-like, were Feathergill's deputies on guard.

Then he was facing northward again, a tall man riding hard, spanning the creeks and choosing for himself the easiest trail whenever a choice was given him. He was glad now that he had ridden this way yesterday and thus had a familiarity with the high country; and he thought, ironically: *Some good came out of it after all*. . . . He took to looking often at the sun, measuring hours and measuring miles, and he grew dissatisfied with the swiftness of time and the slowness of travel and had to fight hard against his reckless desire to keep the horse at a constant punishing pace.

In late afternoon he was in timber, and sight of the valley was shut from him, and shortly he came upon the old stage road winding sinuously down from the higher hills. He had now a new choice to make. He could follow the stage road to Summit House, dropping from there to Circle M and turning directly northward upon the valley's floor to Warbonnet. He could do that, or he could cut downward across the face of the hills in a bee-line for Ordway's spread. He was very careful about his decision, weighing all the factors, comparing a known terrain against the chances of the unknown; and he found then that it was hard to think. His body was weary and his brain was weary, and he wanted nothing so much as to be done with riding.

He chose to go the direct way to Warbonnet, and he crossed the stage road and threaded on through the timber, walking his horse and regretting his decision before he had gone a tortuous mile. He came upon a creek and stopped to give his horse a drink and himself a drink; he had no remembrance of this creek from the old days, but this was country that lay above Warbonnet, and he had never been here that he could recall. He saw this unfamiliarity as a menace to his need; and he grew a little frantic, remembering that the racers below would be long since free of any encumbrance and riding hard and straight to the north. He rode onward, knowing that whatever small edge he had gained this afternoon would be lost by turning back to the stage road. All his thinking was bleak.

He broke out of the timber in the last of the afternoon, coming into one of those long, grassy mountain meadows that were lost back here, and he put the horse down this one as fast as he dared, coming again into timber below the meadow. That stretch of openness had heartened him. When the pine closed around him, and the last sunlight was lost, his thinking grew dark-shadowed again, but presently he came upon a road.

It was a poor road, no more than a pair of crumbled ruts, and there was no reason for a road up here; and for a panicky moment he wondered if he'd got far off his course. Then he understood. This was a road Warbonnet used for pole-cutting excursions into the hills; and realizing this, he put the horse hard down the road, calling now for the last of the mount's reserve, squandering it.

The crowding timber blurred past him, and the light grew less certain. The road was sharply graded, and the horse began to falter; and then Madden burst out into openness, and before him stood Warbonnet's buildings, not half a mile away.

In the grass that lay between, he found a pit-and-mound marker, a hole about three feet deep surrounded by four piles of sod. The sight dredged up a remembrance of the instructions Feathergill had given at the registry booth, and he dismounted, realizing now that the marker indicated the southwest corner of a quarter section. And here he set the stake.

Then he rode on toward the buildings, finding Warbonnet with a deserted air, a few saddlers stomping in the corrals the only signs of life. He turned his spent horse out into one

of the corrals and stripped off the gear and began leading the mount back and forth, cooling
off gradually. He was at this when some
soundless warning drew his gaze to the patio.

Ames Luddington was standing there.
Luddington said, "So you made it."

He was wearing his gray suit, but it had the
disheveled look of having been slept in, and
his face bore a day's stubble. His black sombrero was thumbed back, showing the fullness
of his long, strong face; his eyes had a hard
shine to them.

Once Madden had given thought to how it
would be to stand pitted against this man, and
he knew such a moment now in its fullness.
He said, "You couldn't have been that far out
ahead of the rest of them, Ames."

"You planted a thought in me," Luudding-
ton said. "That first night in Sawtelle, you
claimed you'd come down off Tumbling Wall.
I didn't more than half believe you. Then I
reasoned that if it could be done, I could do it.
Last night I knew that no man could get into
the Beavertail from the south, not with those
surveyors posted. But I had a good many extra
hours to circle around and maneuver to the
top of Tumbling Wall. They weren't watching
that end of the valley."

Madden said, "But first you got Stroud out
of bed and told him how he could keep

Willard out of the race."

Luddington smiled. "Willard was certain to have a fast horse."

Madden remembered Stroud and Pearl and how he had thought of them as wolf and coyote, and he knew now that Reva had been right. Here stood the most formidable enemy of all, and he thought: *Wolf, coyote, and snake!* He moved toward the corral gate. "It didn't do you a bit of good, Ames. I've already staked out this quarter section."

"That's what I thought when I saw you here," Luddington said, his voice flat. "I couldn't find any marker to the north. So now, before I change stakes, I've got to kill you." His hand went under his coat and came out with a gun in it; the gun rocked back against his palm and made its harsh thunder.

Madden felt the airlash of the bullet. He went down to his knee then in the trampled dust, this action instinctive, and he reached for his own gun and found his attempt clumsy. There was just one driving thought in him: he had ridden too hard and too long to lose out now. He willed his fingers to obey and realized then what he'd done to his knuckles in that fight with Stroud. He thought: *This is the finish!* seeing Luddington's carefully calculating eyes, seeing Luddington tilt his gun a second time; despair crowded Madden, and the taste of brass was in his mouth.

That was when he become conscious of Tucker Ordway.

The man stood at the far end of the patio, having come around the ranchhouse; he stood leaning on a cane which he clasped with his left hand; in his right he held a six-shooter. He made a lumpy, awkward figure, his nearly sightless eyes questing, and he lifted his voice and cried, "You! Turn and face me!"

This fetched Luddington about, and Luddington drove a bullet at Ordway, but he had been startled into reckless aiming, and the shot went wide. Only then did Madden understand why Ordway had shouted, inviting death; it was the one means by which Ordway could be sure where Luddington stood. Luddington's movement had told him Luddington's position, and Ordway fired now and fired again, swinging his gun in a great arc.

Madden flattened down hard in the dust, keeping out of the line of fire, and from his position he saw Luddington slowly turn around, then drop his gun. The man bent at the knees and slumped downward, falling full-length upon the patio's flagstones.

Ordway's eyes again quested, and he cried querulously, "Where is he?"

"Dead!" Madden shouted. "Hold your fire."

He came to a stand and strode across the patio and got Ordway's arm. "I'll get you into the house," he said. He led Ordway around the building and up the gallery steps and inside to that great room with the hewn rafters. He eased Ordway into one of the rawhide-bottomed chairs, very mindful of the wound Ordway had got at Summit House.

"There," Madden said. "That does it."

He looked up then and saw that the picture was gone from above the fireplace.

Released tension left Ordway trembling. He said, "First I heard his voice. It wasn't a familiar voice, so I came for a look. When I heard what he was saying, I savvied. I didn't want this race, in spite of all the talking Rex and Corry did. But if there had to be a race, I wanted it a fair one. Who was he?"

"Warbonnet's worst enemy," Madden said. "You can have that to remember."

Ordway sighed and settled deep into his chair. "You were doing something in the corral, I think."

"Cooling off my horse. I staked out this chunk of land for the Willards. Things got fixed so they couldn't ride."

Ordway thought about this, pushing his fingers through his leonine mane. A puzzled man, he said, "I figured you wrong once. Hap Sutton has convinced me of that. But I didn't expect this. Why, Madden?"

"Because I figured you wrong, too." He turned toward the door. "I'll be getting back to that horse."

But only when he came again into the patio and saw the sprawled body of Luddington lying there did the full truth strike him, and he thought then: *Why I owe my life to the old hellion!* He turned the wonder of this over in his mind, and he was never again to think of that whipping. He looked at Luddington and was ashamed of having trusted Luddington and brought him to this range, and there came to him a reflection upon each man doing his own sowing and his own reaping. This brought him a remembrance of Cibo Pearl and a last task as yet undone.

He dragged Luddington's body to the bunkhouse and laid it out. Then he went to finish his work with his horse; before this was done the first of the racers were upon Warbonnet. He heard their lifted shouts out there where he set his stake, but no man showed to contest him. They went whirling away to look for other markers, and he listened to the drumming of hoofs and wished the riders well.

He left his own saddler in the corral and cut out a horse bearing Warbonnet's brand and put his gear on it and was riding down toward

217

the gate within the hour. The gate stood open and unguarded now, and he rode through it in the twilight and faced toward Sawtelle.

17. Gunsmoke

Cibo Pearl sat on one of the crippled chairs in the echoing emptiness of Summit House at dusk on the day of the race, a frightened man showing a day's stubble of beard, his rumpled suit testifying to hasty riding. At his feet was a black satchel, filled and heavy. Out back, his flogged horse stood with drooping head in the stable, but Pearl was not thinking of the horse; it was no more to him than an instrument of escape to be discarded when its usefulness was done.

A restlessness possessed Pearl, and a nervousness that made him start at every scurrying rat, every squeak of this old pile. At last he moved to the doorway and squatted there, looking out upon the stump-dotted clearing. He fetched the black satchel with him and kept it close at hand, not conscious that he was giving it this concern. He was contemplating the position in which he now found himself, and his thoughts were like the twitching movements of shadows, edged with fear.

He had known stark terror from the moment Reva had crumpled to the floor of the Palace the night before. He'd stood there with his smoking derringer in his hand, realizing that he'd brought his world down about him. A man might hang Tucker Ordway's picture over his bar and find those who resented the insult to Ordway; but there would be just as many to share the grim jest, making themselves allies. But when a man had back-shooting blood on his hands, and a woman's blood at that, he could only expect to find all other men against him. There'd been nothing left but to flee.

But first there'd been money to be gathered, some of it in the barroom and some in his quarters; and the money he'd stuffed into his satchel. He'd been at this when Doc Stone had come to the Palace, fetched by the swamper, and together the two had carried the dying Reva away. Damn that swamper for a meddling old fool! He would settle with that one some day! So thinking, Pearl had cowered in his quarters, the derringer ready in his hand, until the two had departed with their burden.

Then he tucked the derringer away and wrapped a gunbelt holding a Colt's forty-five around his thick middle. He might need the gun with the greater carrying power if pursuit took his trail. And pursuit would come; he had been very sure of that.

He kept a horse of his own at the livery; and soon he'd been on the trail, the satchel tied to his saddle and his garish saloon left forever behind him. But before he'd ridden out, he'd looked up one of his hirelings — the only one who might still be of service to him — and given that one instructions and listened to the fellow's suggestion.

Then Pearl had faced a choice of trails, and wisdom had percolated through his terror to make his choice for him. Pursuit would expect him to head along the stage road, either to Yellow Lodge or to the west, and thence out of the country. Instead, he'd taken the old untraveled stage road that climbed the western wall of the Beavertail; and thus he had come through the night here to Summit House.

He had arrived in mid-morning and managed to sleep fitfully for a couple of hours, and then the Peso Kid had come riding into the clearing. The Kid had stepped down and called out cautiously and presented Pearl with a saddlebag holding food enough for a few days.

"Ees *mucho* people in town, *senor*," the Kid had reported. "They have come for the race."

"Madden — ?"

The Kid shrugged. "Him I do not see."

Pearl had been heartened. That land rush would give people something to think about besides a dead singer from Pearl's Palace. They would be racing for land before they raced to put a noose around the neck of Cibo Pearl. He had this much reprieve; and he'd wondered then if he shouldn't use it to pile the miles behind him, building up a barricade of them. But he asked the Kid, "You did as we decided?"

"I hire a *hombre* to pass the word to *Senor* Madden. Eet will be done." The Kid shrugged again. "Is eet wise, bringing him here?"

Pearl shuddered. "The others will ride around in circles for a while, then give up the scent as lost and go about their business. *He* is the one who will never forget Cibo Pearl and never cease hunting. There was something between him and Reva that day you shot him out of his saddle; I'm sure of it. I do not want to be forever looking over my shoulder. Nor do I want to have to jump every time a door opens or a stray rider stirs the dust in whatever town I choose. Yes, Peso, it is wise for a man to insure his sleep."

Yet even then he'd once more had to fight down the desire to be into his saddle and away.

The Kid had made a motion of rubbing his thumb against the index finger of his right hand. "The *dinero, senor.* The *dinero* you promised me for getting the picture and for doing thees little chore for you today."

"Oh, yes," Pearl had said. They were standing in the clearing before the open doorway. "It's in the satchel sitting there on the floor. Help yourself."

The Peso Kid had stepped into the deserted, dusty barroom, Pearl behind him, and the Kid had bent to fumble with the clasp of the satchel, and in that unguarded moment his back was to Pearl. There again Pearl had had a choice, and he'd thought: *Two guns against one at the showdown?* weighing the need for Peso as an ally, balancing this against his own avarice and the knowledge that all he owned in the world was inside that satchel.

He'd used the derringer instead of the six-gun. It made its small sound in the rotting old building, and there was no need for it to speak a second time . . .

He'd dragged the Kid's body out to the back and left it beside the stable, and returned to the clearing to give some thought to Peso's horse. He could have led it into the timber and shot the mount, and it was not mercy that made his choice for him but a fear that someone might have been near enough to hear the first shot and would surely come to investigate if there were a second.

He compromised by leading the horse into the timber, stripping the gear from it and dumping saddle, bridle and blanket into the brush. Then he slapped the horse across the rump and sent it bolting. No one, finding the Kid's horse, would concern himself with the Kid's whereabouts. No one cared that much about the Peso Kid. . . .

All this had been hours before, and now with night settling down over the hills, Pearl was resigned to many more hours of waiting. Had Madden ridden in the race? Then it might not be until tonight or tomorrow that Madden would return to Sawtelle and receive the message the Peso Kid had fashioned for him. Pearl measured the hours and measured the miles and tried to restore himself to calmness, but always at the edge of his consciousness was the remembrance of his plight. It stemmed from that picture he had coveted for so long, and so it came to him that Tucker Ordway had at last driven him from Sawtelle. Ordway had been more formidable in the painting than he'd been in the flesh. But it was not Ordway that Pearl feared now, but a tall man whose tenacity might be Pearl's complete undoing.

And so he waited. The waiting dragged at his nerves until he hated Summit House and ached to be into the saddle and riding. Only then did he really regret killing the Peso Kid, for the hardest part was waiting alone. . . .

Madden rode into Sawtelle on the borrowed Warbonnet saddler late of that same night and went at once to the Ogallala and tumbled into his bed, boneweary. He slept well into the morning and got up and shaved and took his belated breakfast in the dining room; and it was here he heard Stroud's name mentioned and learned that Stroud was dead.

"Tried to sooner into the valley yesterday morning," a man explained, when Madden asked for the details. "One of those surveyors stopped him, and Stroud tried for a gun. He was just a mite slow."

So that was how it had been, and Madden turned the knowledge over in his mind and found nothing surprising about it. That would have been Stroud's way — rough and clumsy, lacking the calculated thoughtfulness that had sent Luddington down off Tumbling Wall. The wolf had been too bold and had died of his boldness. It was finished.

Madden came to the boardwalk and fashioned up a cigarette and stood there, empty of feeling except for his thoughts of Cibo Pearl and the need to be riding. This need had lost its urgency; he had all of his life to trail Pearl, and he had come back to Sawtelle to make his start from here. He looked over the town; it held only the echo of yesterday's excitement, but there were more settlers on the street than were to be found on an ordinary day, and the mercantile seemed to be doing a good business.

Barbed wire, Madden guessed, and was a little sorry. Well, Tucker Ordway wouldn't be able to see it. He would live out his days in his own crowding darkness, his comforts attended to and his only images the old brave ones.

A man shuffled up and asked, "You Madden?"

Madden nodded, vaguely recalling the man as a hanger-on at Pearl's Palace; there were faces like his, aged and lined and lost, in the shadowy corners of every saloon.

"I got a message for you, feller. From Mrs. Willard. She wants you to meet her at Summit House as soon as you can make it."

"So — ?" Madden said and gave the fellow a dollar.

He then walked idly toward the livery stable and found Gunther seated before the doorway, a slumped figure on a bench. He had not seen Gunther since that night up on the switchbacks, and he gave him a nod and went into the stable and saddled up. When he led his horse outside, Gunther was still sitting, and Madden said then, "How did you make out in the race?"

Gunther lifted his shaggy head. "My horse stumbled and broke its leg. Before I'd gone a mile." He showed the patience of one used to fortitude, but a great bewilderment was in his bovine eyes. "I bring the news to all the rest, and I am the one who loses when the race is run. How is that?"

Madden said, "Something you said that night in the hills led me to believe you were kin to that man who died out in the valley."

"My cousin," Gunther said.

"Did he have a family?"

Gunther shook his head. "We were going to farm together, once we found land. My missus liked him."

Madden said, "You know the Circle M spread, south of Warbonnet?"

Gunther nodded.

"Some of it's uphill, but a lot of it can be farmed. I own it, Gunther. I'll never live on it again. It's yours. I'll deed it to you whenever I reach Yellow Lodge."

Gunther's eyes widened, his eyes not believing at first, and then gratitude came into them, and he was voiceless.

Madden pulled himself up into the saddle. "I was the man who shot your cousin, not Willard. I didn't have much choice, Gunther. But I'll sleep better for knowing his kinsman farms my land."

227

Gunther shook his head. "We was fools, all of us. Him and me and all the rest who believed Stroud."

Madden smiled bleakly and touched his thumb to the second button of his shirt. "You had company," he said and neck-reined into the street, heading west.

As he made the climb to where he could look down upon Sawtelle, he was reminded that probably Reva would be buried today; and he wondered if he should have waited for the funeral. But he knew that the homage he would pay would be of a different kind, and it would be paid at Summit House. He had not been deceived by the message that purported to be from Corinna. She would have summoned him to Warbonnet if she'd wanted to see him; a day had made that much difference.

He considered the transparency of the ruse and smiled his bleak smile again. Once since he'd returned to the Beavertail he'd been asked to meet Corinna secretly, and whoever had framed today's message had known of that rendezvous and supposed he would again be drawn by such a lure. Reva had known about that meeting, but Reva was dead. That left the Peso Kid, who'd waited on the hillside above Circle M to do Cibo Pearl's bidding.

Attaining the ridges, Madden rode along

228

them, following the now familiar trail he had ridden twice in the last two days. Again he had his glimpses of the valley below, and he forded the familiar creeks and dipped into the lost mountain meadows and came, when noon was long past, into the timber, finding the old stage road and following it down to the clearing before Summit House. Here he grew wary. Mindful of his slowness yesterday against Luddington, he lifted his gun from leather, testing the resiliency of his hand; then, satisfied, he let the gun slide back into the holster.

A droning afternoon's silence held the clearing; the wind made its soft murmuring in the pine tops, and a hawk wheeled across the sky's endless blue. And Madden stepped down from his saddle and walked toward the open doorway of Summit House, hesitating just outside it, his judgment strong that Pearl was waiting somewhere beyond that doorway, and perhaps the Peso Kid as well.

And then the nauseating reek of Pearl's perfume was so strong in Madden's nostrils that he knew that Pearl stood just behind the door.

He had to smile inwardly at the way Pearl had unwittingly betrayed himself, and then he stepped softly across the ancient threshold and lunged hard against the door, hurling his left shoulder at the rotting wooden panel at the same time that he lifted out his gun with his right hand. The force of the impact knocked Pearl off his feet; the man went scurrying across the floor on hands and knees as Mace Stroud had once done, and Madden leaped after him and set his boot against Pearl and spilled him over.

Then Madden stepped back and looked at the sprawled figure of Pearl, the beard-stubbled face and eyes wide with terror, and the mouth slack and grimacing, and he said, "You're one hell of a specimen, Cibo!"

"I didn't do it!" Pearl shrilled. "I swear I didn't do it!"

Anger swept through Madden. "Stand up and take it!"

But Pearl didn't rise. He had the six-shooter in his hand, and he lifted it. Madden watched the gun come up, giving Pearl all the time in the world. A wild urgency rode Pearl, and a wild desperation; but still Madden waited, time a motionless thing to him, and the silence droning all around. Only when Pearl's eyes told him that the man's finger was tightening on the trigger did Madden fire.

Even then there was a moment when mercy might have ruled him, and in that moment he had time to remember Reva dying and Reva not wanting him to know who had shot her, lest a new hate replace his old one. But this was different, and realizing the difference, he had no regret. What had driven him hard against Ordway had been petty, made of a man's pride and therefore holding selfishness, for it excluded all else. Today he was doing what any man would do, not for himself but because it had to be done in decency's name.

So thinking, he saw Pearl's body jolt to the impact of the bullet. Some last reflex in Pearl put pressure in his finger, and his gun boomed harmlessly, the bullet going overhead. But that was a shot Pearl didn't hear, for he was dead.

Madden at once quested the far corners of the room, his gun held ready, and thus he awaited the Peso Kid. But the last echoes of gun-thunder died, and the last wisp of gun-smoke drifted to oblivion, and the restored silence droned on. Madden looked down at the body of Pearl and slipped his gun into its holster and turned toward the doorway.

18. The Beckoning Trail

Outside, Madden went around to the stable with the thought of turning Pearl's horse loose, and thus he came upon the body of the Peso Kid. He stood looking at the Kid, not sure why the Kid had died but knowing that it must have been Pearl who'd put a bullet in Peso's back. He wasted little time on speculation; it didn't matter about the Kid. The Kid was another who'd sowed and reaped.

Turning Pearl's horse loose, Madden then went rummaging about the stable until he came upon a discarded shovel. It was rusted badly and the handle had nearly rotted away, but with it he was able to lift the sod loam near the stable, scooping out a shallow grave into which he got both Pearl and the Kid. He stood contemplating the grave afterward, and it came to him that there was nothing more to do. Nothing.

He had noticed Pearl's satchel in Summit House. Now he went back inside and had a look in the satchel and whistled softly. He took the satchel and Pearl's saddlebag with him.

After that he caught up his horse and went riding along the old stage road, feeling weary, feeling empty, and presently he got out of timber and could look down into the valley. Here, in the last light, he could see smoke lifting at many places. These were the supper fires of the new homesteaders; the smoke of the tent city had been transplanted to the valley and was now scattered to far-flung improvised hearths. It made a comforting sight, banishing loneliness, but the homesteaders' way was not for him. Soon the crimson and gold of autumn would climb into the evergreen of the hills, and that meant the axes would ring and the stout walls would go up against the winter. Another year and there would be a schoolhouse in the Beavertail, and roads, and wire. He thought of Circle M and its graze turning to Gunther's plow, and he knew that he would never come to the valley again.

Reaching the Beavertail's floor, he rode aimlessly, heading in the general direction of Sawtelle until suddenly he wanted no more of Sawtelle and that room in the Ogallala where he had spent so many futile hours. His own saddlebag was there, but he had Pearl's, and he could pay his hotel bill by mail. So thinking, he came upon the southbound trail and sat his saddle here, in no hurry to go anywhere, and it was then he saw a rider coming along the trail, leading an extra horse. He recognized Corinna as she drew close; the extra horse was his own.

She drew rein. "Hello, Larry," she said. "I was going into town to return your horse."

He said, "And I've been thinking about taking this one to Warbonnet. We can make the switch right here." He got down from his saddle and dragged off the gear and transferred it to his own mount. He held Pearl's satchel in his hand, then passed it to Corinna, keeping the saddlebag with its food. "I'll be obliged if you'll take care of this. It belonged to Pearl. He's dead. You heard about Reva?"

"Yesterday morning," she said, and her face softened. "We'd found Dad's picture missing from the house, and we reasoned that the Peso Kid must have stolen it. The rest of the story was told us by a saloon swamper. Reva destroyed the picture, which Pearl had hung in his bar. That must be why Pearl shot her."

Madden remembered the picture's being missing at Warbonnet yesterday, and now he understood about Reva, and he thought: *Why, she believed what she preached enough to die for it!* and he felt humble.

Corinna said, "So much has happened.

Reva. You, and Dad, and that man Luddington." She took the satchel. "What shall I do
with this?"

"Turn it over to the law when a new deputy
is appointed. Wearing the badge will be a good
job for Willard. It won't take much of his
time. He'll still be able to do his ranching."

Corinna said, "Feathergill claims there
shan't be any trouble about your riding for us
by proxy. He'll fix that. And we needn't worry
about that charge against Rex. Those who
might have pushed it are gone — Stroud and
Pearl and Medwick and Barker." She lifted
her eyes to him and was a small girl over-
whelmed with feeling. "We've so very much
to thank you for, Larry."

He shrugged. He looked to the north where
Tumbling Wall glimmered whitely at the valley's end, and he held silent.

"And now, Larry — ?" she asked.

"I'll ride out," he said. "Tonight." He extended his hand. "I guess that makes this
good-bye, Corry."

She reined close to him and lifted her face;
it held all its old sweetness, and her eyes
would learn to laugh again. He had done that
for her, and it was a good thing to see; it was
his reward, and it was enough.

She said, "I wish that you would kiss me
before you go, Larry."

The old hunger leaped up in him, making a mad moment when nothing else counted so much, but he had this wisdom in him: he knew there could be no bridging back to the yesterdays, and he knew with what faith her offer was made. He said, "I've never wanted anything that belonged to another man, Corry. You can tell him that, if you wish. Take care of him. And take care of Tuck Ordway. They are both going to need you."

She looked close to crying; she was sad and joyous at the same time. She said, "Some day, Larry, you are going to find the girl for you. And she is going to be a very lucky girl."

He had never given any thought to this; he had been too concerned with his own petty quest, but he supposed it could be true; and now, suddenly, it came to him that he would know this girl when he met her. She would be part Corinna and part Reva, owning some of the beauty of each, and some of the courage. And he wondered then where he would meet her and when, in what strange town, around what strange corner.

Corinna said, "Is there anything I can do for you, Larry?"

"Yes," he said. "You can keep Reva's grave green."

She said very solemnly, "I'll do that. She was my friend, too."

"I'll be riding now," he said and touched spurs to his horse. He lifted it to a gallop and headed northward.

For a while he rode at full tilt, the wind in his face and the saddle rocking beneath him. He paralleled Warbonnet's wire and found it down, the barrier leveled by the rushing entrymen. Then as he drew nearer to the north end of the valley, the land began to tilt upward; and he had to slow the horse. Presently, when he'd attained a rise, he drew rein and turned in his saddle, looking back down upon the Beavertail, knowing that this was his last look.

He thought of all that had happened here and considered then what had come of it: he had found himself. Free of hate, he had become a free man. He thought of Reva, who had understood how that might be; he remembered her wanting his life to be a good life. He thought of the beckoning trail ahead and dedicated it to her.

First he would have to go to Frisco and straighten out his affairs with Ames Luddington's office. Then he'd have a look in at the mine in Arizona. Mining was not for him, so he would leave the running of it to his hirelings and go searching for a ranch somewhere, a ranch he could buy, a place where he could sink down roots. He was fired with the thought of the ranch; he would make of it a friendly place, bright with laughter; he would make it a monument.

There was that business at Yellow Lodge, too; he had to sign over the Circle M to Gunther. He was warmed by that notion; he had found a key to endeavor: you spread yourself around and that made you as big as all the land, and as good. But this wasn't the way to Yellow Lodge, not the direct way. He'd have to circle back.

But now he knew what had faced him in this direction, for Tumbling Wall now loomed above him. Once he'd come down that wall, but afterwards Ames Luddington had made the same descent. But no man had ever climbed Tumbling Wall, not in the memory of the Beavertail, and that was his strong need now, to climb where no other man had climbed, to reach always upward, keeping the sun in his face and his eyes smiling. He would base at the foot of the cliff, and tomorrow morning, early, he would start.

He had to smile at the notion as childish, yet the need was no less compelling. Thus he faced upward and became a tall man riding upward, unafraid of the trail, glad of the tomorrow.

THORNDIKE PRESS hopes you have enjoyed this Large Print book. All our Large Print titles are designed for easy reading, and all our books are made to last. Other Thorndike Large Print books are available at your library, through selected bookstores, or directly from the publisher. For more information about current and upcoming titles, please call or mail your name and address to:

THORNDIKE PRESS
PO Box 159
Thorndike, Maine 04986
800/223-6121
207/948-2962